VANDERBILT MEMORIAL HOSPITAL MEDICAL NOTES

PATIENT: TOM FLYNT
ATTENDING NURSE: TINA WHITE

- Patient Flynt set to be released; still has no memories of who he is.

- Wounds to head have healed rapidly.

- Fast progress due to patient's incredible physique and remarkable fitness.

- Could invite patient over for Thanksgiving meal—no use in us both being alone for the holiday.

- Am supposed to be taking care of patient—why do I feel like he's trying to take care of me…?

Dear Reader,

The 20th anniversary excitement continues as we bring you a 2-in-1 collection containing brand-new novellas by two of your favorite authors: Maggie Shayne and Marilyn Pappano. *Who Do You Love?* It's an interesting question—made more complicated for these heroes and heroines because they're not quite what they seem, making the path to happily-ever-after an especially twisty one. Enjoy!

A YEAR OF LOVING DANGEROUSLY continues with *Her Secret Weapon* by bestselling writer Beverly Barton. This is a great secret-baby story—with a forgotten night of passion thrown in to make things even more exciting. Our in-line 36 HOURS spin-off continues with *A Thanksgiving To Remember,* by Margaret Watson. Suspenseful and sensual, this story shows off her talents to their fullest. Applaud the return of Justine Davis with *The Return of Luke McGuire.* There's something irresistible about a bad boy turned hero, and Justine's compelling and emotional handling of the theme will win your heart. In *The Lawman Meets His Bride,* Meagan McKinney brings her MATCHED IN MONTANA miniseries over from Desire with an exciting romance featuring a to-die-for hero. Finally, pick up *The Virgin Beauty* by Claire King and discover why this relative newcomer already has people talking about her talent.

Share the excitement—and come back next month for more!

Leslie J. Wainger
Executive Senior Editor

Please address questions and book requests to:
Silhouette Reader Service
U.S.: 3010 Walden Ave., P.O. Box 1325, Buffalo, NY 14269
Canadian: P.O. Box 609, Fort Erie, Ont. L2A 5X3

A THANKSGIVING
TO REMEMBER

MARGARET WATSON

Published by Silhouette Books

America's Publisher of Contemporary Romance

For Mom.
Thanks for believing in me and being my biggest fan.

Special thanks and acknowledgment are given
to Margaret Watson for her contribution
to the 36 Hours series.

 SILHOUETTE BOOKS

ISBN 0-373-27105-0

A THANKSGIVING TO REMEMBER

Visit Silhouette at www.eHarlequin.com

Printed in U.S.A.

Books by Margaret Watson

Silhouette Intimate Moments

An Innocent Man #636
An Honorable Man #708
To Save His Child #750
The Dark Side of the Moon #779
*Rodeo Man #873
*For the Children #886
*Cowboy with a Badge #904
*The Fugitive Bride #920
The Marriage Protection Program #951
Family on the Run #988
A Thanksgiving To Remember #1035

*Cameron, Utah

MARGARET WATSON

From the time she learned to read, Margaret could usually be found with her nose in a book. Her lifelong passion for reading led to her interest in writing, and now she's happily writing exactly the kind of stories she likes to read. Margaret is a veterinarian who lives in the Chicago suburbs with her husband and their three daughters. In her spare time she enjoys rollerblading, bird-watching and spending time with her family. Readers can write to Margaret at P.O. Box 2333, Naperville, IL 60567-2333.

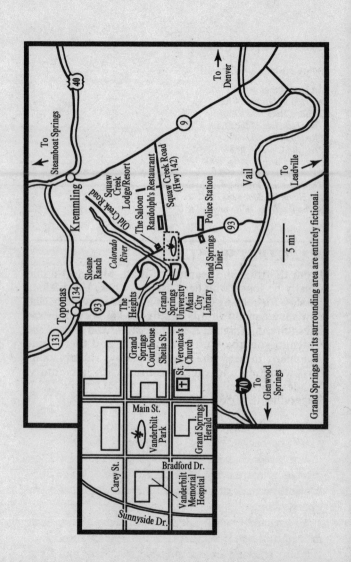

Grand Springs and its surrounding area are entirely fictional.

Chapter 1

"I need help here, White!"

The bark of the doctor's voice cut through the din of the emergency room and nurse Tina White looked up from the patient she was bandaging. "I'll be right there," she called.

She looked down at the woman lying on the table with an encouraging smile. "You're going to be fine," she said, her voice low and reassuring. "You heard what the doctor said. Your wrist is only sprained, and although it will hurt for a few days, you'll be back to normal before you know it."

She applied the last piece of tape and eased the woman's injured arm back onto the table. "The doctor will be back in a moment, and she'll probably let you go home."

Giving the woman another reassuring smile, Tina moved to the next cubicle. The emergency room doctor was working on an unconscious man, and Tina moved to the other side of the exam table. Her stomach clenched as she looked at the blood that covered his face and the left side of his head. "Surely he didn't get these injuries in the chaos at the masquerade ball earlier this evening?" she asked, moving instinctively to staunch the flow of blood from the man's head.

"Car accident," the doctor answered tersely as he examined the patient. "The police said he was one of two men who ran out of the hotel when the lights went out."

Tina raised her head and looked over at the doctor. "What was he doing?"

The doctor shrugged. "Who knows? Maybe he was the guy who fired the shots. We won't know anything until he wakes up."

Tina looked down at the man who lay so silent and still on the table. His short, dark brown hair was disheveled and his face was pale and streaked with blood, but something about his features tugged at Tina. "He doesn't look like a criminal."

The doctor snorted. "Most criminals don't." His hands moved over the patient, gentle yet probing. "No matter who he is, he's one lucky guy. That cut on his head is going to need suturing and it feels like he might have a couple of broken ribs and a concussion, but other than that he looks like he's going to be all right."

Tina pressed on the gauze pad she was holding over the wound on the man's head, holding it more firmly to slow the bleeding. "What do you want me to do?"

The doctor raked his eyes over the patient, giving him an assessing look that Tina recognized. Then he said, "Get him cleaned up so I can suture that cut. Our first priority is to stop that bleeding. Then start another bag of fluids. The first one is almost finished."

They worked in silence for the next half hour. The doctor occasionally muttered a request to Tina, but she usually anticipated his needs and handed him an instrument before he asked. When the doctor finally stepped back, there was a neat line of sutures along the left side of the stranger's head.

"Get that bandaged, then we'll get him into X-ray and get a scan of his head and chest. I want to make sure there isn't any other damage."

Tina gently covered the wound with bandage and tape, then hovered over their unconscious patient, reluctant to leave him alone. "Is there anyone with him?"

"The paramedics told me he was alone in the car. I have no idea if the police have managed to locate his family." He looked around the emergency room, where the chaos that had reigned earlier was beginning to subside. "It looks like things have quieted down a little." He shook his head. "I don't think this is the way most of these people planned to spend their Halloween." He glanced around again. "Can you take this one over to X-ray, or should I call an orderly?"

Tina didn't tell the doctor that her shift on another floor of the hospital had ended several hours ago, or that she had volunteered to help in the busy emergency room. "Don't bother with an orderly," she said at once. "I'll take him."

The doctor helped her load the man onto a gurney, then she wheeled him out of the emergency room and over to the X-ray department. The technician glanced briefly down at the patient, then looked back at Tina. "Another one from the Steele ball?"

"Car accident," she said, handing him the papers the emergency-room doctor had filled out. "He needs a scan of his head and chest."

The technician looked at the papers and frowned. "These don't have any insurance information. We need that before we can get started."

Tina's temper flared. "You know that's not true in an emergency," she said, her voice cold. "He was alone in the car and the police haven't brought his ID in yet. I'm sure you'll get the information as soon as it's available. But we need that scan now."

The technician gave her patient a dubious glance, then shrugged. "If you say so. All I do is fill out the paperwork."

Tina smoothed a protective hand over the bandage on the unconscious man's head as she struggled to control her temper.

He came around the desk to help her push the gurney into a cubicle. "They're not exactly standing in line here at two in the morning."

Tina stood in the waiting room while the technician performed the tests on her patient, pacing from one side to the other. "What's the matter with you?" she muttered to herself. "This guy is just another patient."

But he wasn't just another patient. For some reason, Tina felt unusually protective toward the unnamed man. Maybe it was because he was completely helpless and alone, no one waiting anxiously for him in the waiting room, no one to hold his hand as he lay unconscious. Or maybe it was because of the doctor's quick, careless assumption that he was a criminal.

Or maybe it was because she found him attractive. She forced herself to face the truth. Even though his face was pasty-white and a bandage covered half his head, he was still a very handsome man. Thick eyelashes fanned out against his pale cheeks. His face was lean, but there were lines around his eyes that told her he smiled frequently. She wondered what color those eyes were, wondered if she would see kindness or indifference in them when he woke up.

It didn't matter, she told herself, appalled at the direction her thoughts were taking. She didn't moon over men she was nursing. She was a professional, dedicated to giving her patients the best care she possibly could. And as a professional, she didn't get involved with her patients, either.

Thank goodness she had remembered that, she told herself firmly.

The door to the X-ray cubicle opened and the technician wheeled out the gurney. "Here's your boy," he said, maneuvering the gurney into place next to the desk.

"What did you find?" Tina found herself leaning toward the technician, her heart pounding.

The technician shrugged. "I have no idea. The radiologist has been busy tonight and it'll be a while before he gets to your scans. A lot of people got hurt in that mess at the Steeles' ball. After David and Lisa Steele got themselves shot, everyone panicked and tried to get out at the same time. They're still getting people into the emergency room."

"You're right. I just thought you might have taken a look."

The technician shook his head. "I put them in the box for the doc to look at. He'll get to them as soon as he can."

"All right." Tina swallowed her disappointment. The technician wasn't the one who would diagnose any problems, anyway. "I'll go ahead and take him up to his room."

The unnamed man lay still and unmoving as Tina pushed the heavy gurney to the elevator, then rolled him into the room he'd been assigned. She was absurdly happy that he was on the floor where she usually worked. His breathing was steady and regular as she hooked him up to the monitors that would keep track of his vital signs. Finally, when she was finished, she stood back and looked at him for a moment.

Lights flashed and blinked, and a low, steady hum seemed to fill the room. The numbers on the monitor attached to his intravenous line glowed at her, and she looked around at the stark, cheerless room. Anyone who woke up alone in a hospital room would be frightened and confused.

She didn't want this man to wake up with only machines for company. Although her legs ached after working for more than twelve hours and her tired eyes were gritty and hot, she sat down in the chair next to the bed.

She'd only been there for a few minutes when someone walked into the room. Tina turned around and faced a beefy man in a slightly-too-small suit who walked over to the bed and stared down at her patient.

"Is he awake yet?"

She jumped up from her chair and stepped between

the man and her patient, and the man took a step backward. "Who are you?" she demanded.

He pulled a wallet out of the inner pocket of his suit jacket and flashed a badge at her. "Detective Bob Jones, Grand Springs Police Department." He held the badge in front of her nose long enough for her to read it, then snapped the wallet shut and replaced it in his pocket. He nodded toward the bed. "Is he awake?"

"No, he's still unconscious," Tina answered.

Bob Jones peered around her at the man on the bed, as if he suspected she wasn't telling him the truth. "How long before he wakes up?"

"No one knows," she said coolly. "And when he does wake up, it may be a while before you can question him."

The detective glanced over at her, and Tina felt him assessing her. Finally he nodded. "I'll talk to his doctor," he said, his voice dismissive.

"He'll tell you the same thing." Tina lifted her chin into the air.

The detective shrugged. "We'll see."

Tina glanced behind her, but her patient was still unconscious. "Have you found out who he was and located his family?" she asked.

"We found his driver's license. His name is Tom Flynt. We're trying to locate his family, but so far no luck." He looked at her more intently. It felt like a laser had suddenly swung around on her. "Has he said anything to you?"

"He's been unconscious since the paramedics brought him into the ER," she said.

The detective's gaze was penetrating as he watched

her. "There's something else you ought to know about this guy," he said after a moment.

Tina bristled at the way the detective referred to her patient as "this guy."

"What's that?"

Jones nodded at the man lying on the hospital bed. "The paramedics found a gun in a holster, strapped to his back."

Tina felt her stomach swoop away from her. "What does that mean?"

"I've got no idea. But since David and Lisa Steele were shot and killed tonight and he ran out of the ball, it makes me very interested in talking to Mr. Flynt." He paused, and his shrewd gaze raked over her again, pausing at her name tag. "Keep that in mind, Ms. White. And let me know when he wakes up."

He turned and walked out the door without looking back.

Tina listened to his footsteps fade away, then sank back down in the chair next to the bed. "Who are you?" she whispered, watching his face.

But he didn't move, didn't respond. She would have to wait until he woke up for answers, just like everyone else. "At least we know your name now," she said. "Your name is Tom. Tom Flynt."

She watched for some sign that he had heard her, some glimmer of recognition, but there was nothing. Sighing, she leaned forward and rested her arms on the bed rail. "You can wake up anytime now," she said. "Everyone wants to know what you were doing at the ball, and why you ran out of the hotel. Why were you there, Tom Flynt? Were you chasing a killer?"

Her voice was low in the darkened room, but her attention was focused completely on her patient. "I don't think you shot the Steeles," she murmured. "You don't look like a criminal."

She blushed when she heard her words, wondering where they had come from. It was too late and she was too tired, she told herself. It made her speak before she thought. But it didn't matter. No one else could hear her, least of all the unconscious Tom Flynt.

Better, though, to concentrate on her job. His right hand was curled slightly, and she took his fingers gently in hers. "You don't want to crimp your IV line," she said softly. Even though he couldn't hear her, it felt right to talk to him, to let him know he wasn't alone. "The night nurse wouldn't like it if she had to get someone up here to start another IV."

She tried to straighten his fingers, but his hand curled around hers and held her lightly. His large hand engulfed her much smaller one, cradling it gently. Warmth stole up her arm. Absurdly, she felt like he was reassuring her. And protecting her. Heat flared in her face as she stared at the unknown man.

"I'm supposed to be taking care of you," she murmured, leaning forward and looking into his face. "Why do I feel like you're trying to take care of me?" She wondered if it had anything to do with the murders at the masquerade ball. "Everyone is safe now, including you. You're going to be fine."

He didn't answer, of course. He lay motionless and silent, but he didn't let go of her hand.

It was the darkest part of the night and he was alone, so instead of pulling away, Tina curled her fingers around his hand and squeezed gently. No one would ever know, she told herself, including her mystery patient. There was no need to hurry back to the emergency room. Most of the patients were already taken care of, and she was supposed to be off duty, anyway.

"Let me tell you what we did for you tonight, Mr. Flynt," she said, her low voice surrounding them in the semidarkness of the hospital room. "You had a car accident," she began. She spoke slowly and calmly, knowing he couldn't hear her words, but hoping that the sound of her voice would somehow comfort him. He didn't let go of her hand, and Tina felt an invisible connection growing between them in the quiet of the impersonal hospital room.

That was absurd, of course. He was simply a patient, and she was only his nurse.

But she continued to talk to him, pausing frequently to look over the machines and make sure his pulse and heartbeat and respiration were normal. The floor nurse looked into the room a few times, but Tina waved her away.

Finally, as the first few streaks of dawn were appearing on the horizon outside the window, the floor nurse came into the room one last time.

"What are you still doing here, Tina?" she asked.

Tina eased her hand away from her patient's and turned around to face the other nurse. "Keeping him company. It always bothers me when we have patients who don't have any family."

The other nurse's face softened. "Yeah, I know what you mean. But didn't your shift end at eleven last night?"

"I went down to the emergency room to help out.

They were really swamped with patients who had been at the Steele masquerade ball.''

"I heard about that." The other nurse frowned. "Is it true that David and Lisa Steele were killed?"

"It's true. And apparently the killer got away."

"Was this guy hurt at the ball?" The nurse gestured at the patient in the bed.''

"No, he was in a car accident. He might have been chasing the man who shot the Steeles."

The other nurse's eyes opened wide. "Was he with the killer?"

"Why would you think that?" Fatigue sharpened Tina's voice, and she struggled to steady it. "I have no idea. I'm sure he'll be able to tell us when he wakes up."

The other nurse gave the man an assessing look. "He looks pretty stable right now. You'd better go home and get some sleep, Tina. With all these patients, we're going to need you back at work later today."

"You're right." Tina glanced at Tom Flynt one more time, then turned away. "I'll be back for my shift this afternoon." She hesitated, then asked, "Is Detective Jones still out there?"

"He sure is. He strikes me as the kind who doesn't give up easily."

"Don't let him bully you."

The other nurse grinned at her. "I'd like to see him try."

Tina smiled back. "That's what I figured you would say, Jenny." And that's why she'd mentioned it. Now it would be a point of honor for Jenny to protect Tom Flynt.

She wanted to ask Jenny to have someone call her

if the man's condition changed, but she stopped herself just in time. She must really be tired, she thought as she stood up, to think about lowering her guard too far and showing her feelings. It was a good thing she was going home. Maybe by the time she returned in the afternoon, she would have reassembled the careful barrier she kept around her emotions.

She allowed herself one last look at Tom Flynt's still form lying on the bed before she turned and left the room.

Tina slept lightly, waking up more than once from a disturbing dream. She told herself that it was merely because of the many injured people she had helped treat the night before, but too many of the dreams featured the still, unconscious face of Tom Flynt, their mystery patient. Finally, at mid-morning, she flung the blankets off the bed and gave up trying to sleep.

She puttered around the house in the bright sunshine. It was hard to believe it was the first of November, but she knew the air would hold a bite of winter when she stepped outside. Already there was snow in the mountains surrounding the town, and it wouldn't be long before they had snow in Grand Springs.

Tina did her morning chores automatically, then sat down to read her newspaper and drink a cup of coffee. The newspaper was full of stories about Jonathan Steele's masquerade ball and the murders of his brother David and sister-in-law Lisa. Finally, Tina closed the paper and went upstairs to get dressed. She was too restless to stay at home until her shift started. Besides, with all the patients who had been admitted the night before, they probably needed extra hands to help out.

"Face it," she told herself, "you just want to get back to the hospital to see Tom Flynt."

Of course she wanted to see how her patient was doing, she thought defensively. She had spent a great deal of time with him the night before. It was only natural to be curious.

But her interest was far more than curiosity. Here in the safety of her own house, she could admit it. Tom Flynt had fascinated her. And the fact that he had been carrying a gun only compounded her interest.

"I don't know what's wrong with you," she scolded herself, as she pulled on a clean white uniform. "You, of all people, should know enough to stay away from a man with a gun."

But it didn't matter. She was suddenly in a fever of anticipation to get back to the hospital and see if Tom Flynt had woken up, and how he was doing. Once he was awake, her interest would end, she told herself. Once she'd talked to him, she'd see he was an ordinary man, just like all the others. And on top of that, a man who carried a gun.

She drove through Grand Springs, marveling at the fact that everything looked so normal. There was no trace of the chaos and tragedy that had struck the town the night before. It looked like the peaceful, quiet place it had been since the last disaster, a blackout, had hit the town several years earlier.

When she arrived at the hospital, a couple of hours early for her shift, she hurried to her floor. She almost swept past the nursing desk, but stopped herself just in time. She paused and smiled at the harried-looking nurse reading a file.

"Hi, Sue," she said, and the nurse looked up at her.

"Oh, hi, Tina," she answered, surprise in her voice. "What are you doing here? You're on afternoons, aren't you?"

"Yes, but I figured we'd be busy so I thought I'd come in early."

Sue's face relaxed in a grateful smile. "That's great. Thanks. We've been running all day. We can always count on you, Tina."

Tina nodded in the direction of Tom's room, hoping her interest looked casual. "I took care of Tom Flynt, the man with the concussion. How's he doing?"

Sue grabbed Tom's chart and glanced at it. "About the same, it looks like."

"Is he still unconscious?"

"As far as I know."

Tina nodded. "I think I'll look in on him, as long as I'm here."

Tina hurried away from the desk and stepped into Tom's room. It was much brighter in the light of day, and the sunlight slanted off his face, making his beard look dark and heavy. It didn't look like he'd moved since she had left a few hours before.

She stood watching him for a moment, then sat down in the chair that still stood next to his bed. "Hi, Tom," she said in a low voice, as she watched him. "I just stopped by to see how you were doing before I reported in to work."

As she spoke to him, she thought she saw him stir. She paused for a moment, then spoke again, in the same low voice. "Are you getting ready to wake up? It's all right. You're safe now, and there are a lot of people here to help take care of you."

This time he definitely moved, and Tina's hands tightened on the bed rail. She saw his throat muscles ripple as he swallowed once, then his eyes fluttered open.

Her first thought was that he had beautiful eyes. They were light brown, the color of well-aged whiskey. When she realized what she was thinking, she shook her head. What was the matter with her?

She leaned toward the bed. "Hello, Tom," she said in a low voice. "How do you feel?"

He looked up at her, a puzzled look on his face. "Who are you? Where am I? What's going on?"

It wasn't unusual for accident victims not to recall their accident once they recovered consciousness. "You had a car accident last night, just outside Grand Springs city limits. You're at Vanderbilt Memorial Hospital, and you're going to be fine." She smiled down at him and lightly touched his hand. "The doctor can tell you exactly what's wrong with you, but you have a cut on your head that we sutured, and you had a concussion. Hold on a minute, I want to get the doctor."

She hurried out of the room and down to the desk. "Sue, Tom Flynt just woke up. Will you call the doctor? I'll go back and stay with him."

Without waiting for an answer, Tina hurried back to the hospital room. Tom Flynt was trying to sit up, and Tina eased him back onto the bed. "Why don't you wait until the doctor gets here before you try to get up? He's going to want to take a good look at you, Mr. Flynt."

He stared at her, and she saw the confusion in his eyes, and the growing fear. "I don't understand," he whispered, his voice harsh and scratchy. "What car accident? What's Grand Springs? And who is Tom Flynt?"

Chapter 2

Without pausing to think, Tina took his hand again. This time, his fingers curled around hers, holding on with an intensity that almost hurt.

"You're Tom Flynt," she said gently. "That's your name."

He frowned up at her. "That doesn't sound familiar."

"You had a car accident. Do you remember anything about that?"

She watched him thinking, then he began to shake his head. He stopped immediately, pain creasing his face. "No. I don't remember anything about a car accident."

"That's not unusual. The mind often blocks out traumatic memories. Many people who have been in an accident can't remember what happened."

"What did you say my name was?"

"Tom Flynt." She waited to see if there was any recognition in his eyes. There wasn't.

"What was the name of the town?" he asked.

"Grand Springs. In Colorado," she added.

She saw the fear creeping into his eyes. "Do I live here?"

"I have no idea, Mr. Flynt. The police haven't told me."

"Police?" The tone of his voice changed, became more urgent. "Why are the police involved?"

"Because of the car accident," she said patiently. "They're investigating it."

She saw him frown again, as if he were trying to concentrate. "There's something I need to remember."

"Don't worry about it, Mr. Flynt," she said. "Your memories will probably come back very soon." She heard a noise at the door, and turned to see Dr. Steve Wilson standing there.

"Good morning, Dr. Wilson."

"Hi, Tina." The doctor gave her a quick smile, then looked past her to the patient on the bed. "I understand that Mr. Flynt has woken up."

Tina reluctantly let go of Tom's hand, then stepped aside. "Just now." She didn't want to examine why she was reluctant to break contact with her patient.

Steve Wilson sat down in the chair next to the bed and talked to Tom Flynt for a while. Then he stood up and examined him. He made some notes on Tom's chart, then sat down again.

"You've had a concussion, Mr. Flynt, and two cracked ribs. One of the fractured ribs abraded a lung, and although the bleeding into your chest was minimal and appears to have stopped, we'll need to keep you in the hospital for a few days to let it heal. All in all, though, I'd say you were darned lucky."

Tom Flynt watched the doctor steadily. "I didn't recognize my name, or the name of this town."

Steve nodded. "You've got amnesia. It's not uncommon after head injuries and traumatic events like car accidents, but your memory seems to be totally gone, which is more unusual. I'm confident it will return, but it might take a few days. And just in case, I'm going to have a specialist take a look at you."

He turned to Tina. "Let me know if anything changes," he said. "I'll be in later."

Tina noticed that Tom watched Steve Wilson carefully as he left the room. When he had disappeared down the hall, Tom looked back at her. "He seems distracted. Do you know why?"

Tina was stunned. "For someone who can't remember his name, you're certainly perceptive. And if he's distracted, it has nothing to do with you. Steve is having some problems at home right now."

Tom nodded. "I thought something was wrong."

"It hasn't affected his work. He's a great doctor," she said quickly. "And everything he said was correct."

"Don't worry, I believe him. It's hard to argue that I don't have amnesia when I can't remember my name." He gave her a wry smile.

His brown eyes were warm and glowing, and, just as she had thought, the lines around his eyes crinkled when he smiled. Her stomach swooped and dipped, and she tightened her grip on the bed rail.

"Do you have any questions I could answer?" she asked hurriedly.

"Can I look in a mirror?" he asked.

"Of course." She found a hand mirror in the bathroom and handed it to him.

Tom took the mirror with the same sensation of unreality that had enveloped him since he'd woken up to see the nurse smiling down at him. He stared at the face in the mirror for a long time, but it looked utterly foreign to him, as unfamiliar as the name "Tom Flynt." He struggled to beat back the panic that threatened to overwhelm him. Finally, he handed the mirror back to the nurse who stood next to the bed. He noticed that his hand was shaking.

"I don't look familiar at all."

"It's all right," she said quietly. "Don't try to force yourself to remember. That will only make it worse."

Tom stared at her bright blue eyes and the rich, dark red of her hair. "You haven't told me your name."

"I'm Tina. Tina White," she said.

He turned the name over in his mind, but it didn't sound familiar, either. Fear clawed at him again, its dark fangs waiting to devour him. He closed his eyes, forcing the monster to recede, until there was nothing inside him at all. His mind felt like a huge black void, totally empty. Except for this woman's voice.

He grasped at the one familiar thing he'd found. "Did I know you before...before the accident?" he asked.

"No." She shook her head. "We never met before last night."

"But your voice sounds familiar to me. It's the only thing that feels familiar."

To his surprise, he saw her face turn a delicate shade of pink. "I think that's because I was talking to you last night. You were unconscious, but I didn't know how much you might be able to hear. And you were alone. So I...talked to you.''

"You did?" As he watched her, fascinated, her cheeks turned a deeper shade of red.

"We always encourage family members to talk to unconscious patients," she said, her voice prim. He watched her try to regain her composure. "It can't hurt, and we think it might help. So I talked to you.''

"And I remembered," he said slowly.

"On some level, I guess you do." Tina moved around the room, keeping her back to him, straightening the already-straight machines that surrounded his bed.

"I definitely remember your voice."

"Then I guess you weren't as deeply unconscious as we'd feared." She turned to face him again and pasted what looked like a professionally detached smile on her face. "Maybe that means your memory will come back quickly, also."

The reminder about his memory jogged something deep in his brain. A sense of urgency surfaced, made more frantic by the fact that he couldn't remember why.

"I need to remember something," he said suddenly.

"Don't worry, Mr. Flynt. It will come back." Tina's voice was once again warm and soothing.

"No, there's something specific. Something I need to do." He moved restlessly, ignoring the stabbing pain in his left side and the pounding in his head. "Maybe if I got up and walked around, I would remember."

"You can't do that," Tina said, moving closer to

the bed. Her blue eyes stared down at him, full of concern and understanding. "I know it's hard, but you're going to have to stay in bed for a while and let your lung heal. And your head." She hesitated, then leaned forward. "I can't imagine what it would be like to forget everything, including who you are. It must be horrible. You must feel so helpless and alone. But we'll do everything we can to help you heal. And I know the police are trying to find out more about you. Chances are we'll have your family standing next to your bed in a few hours."

She hesitated, then said, "Do you think you have a wife, or children?"

"No," he said immediately, then frowned. "I don't know if that's true or not. But I don't feel married."

Her mouth curled into a slow smile, and he couldn't stop staring at her. His heart began racing, and it had nothing to do with his injuries. Tina's whole face seemed to light up when she smiled. "I've heard that line before," she said.

For the first time since he'd woken up, Tom relaxed. "Yeah, I guess you probably have. But it's true—I don't feel married." He smiled at her. "But then, I don't feel like my name is Tom Flynt, and I've never heard of Grand Springs, Colorado, either."

Tina nodded. "I'm sure the detective will be back to talk to you today. He came by last night, when you were still unconscious."

Hearing that the police would come by took away his smile and brought the urgency back. Tina must have seen the change, because she sat down and leaned toward him. "What is it?"

"I don't know. But whenever you mention the police, I get this sense of urgency. Like there's something I should know."

He saw her hesitate, saw her knuckles whiten on the metal rail of his bed. "I'll tell you what happened last night, what led up to your accident, at least as far as we know. Maybe that will help you to remember."

"You don't have to do that, Ms. White. I'll talk to Mr. Flynt."

Detective Bob Jones stood in the doorway, looking at her. Assessing her.

She raised her chin. "Mr. Flynt has amnesia, Detective. He can't remember anything, including his name."

The detective looked over at him, and Tom could see the hard cynicism in his eyes. "That's convenient."

"It's the truth," Tina said hotly. "You can ask Dr. Wilson. He was in here just a few minutes ago."

"Don't worry, I'll talk to the doc," said Detective Jones. "But first I want to talk to Mr. Flynt, here."

Tina moved over to stand next to him. It almost looked as if she were trying to protect him. "You can talk to him for a while, Detective. But he's got serious injuries and I won't let you badger him."

"I don't badger anyone," the detective said, but he was watching Tom instead of Tina. "I just ask questions."

"Ask away," said Tom.

The detective studied him for a while, and Tom stared back. There was nothing familiar about the older man's face. "Do I know you?" Tom finally asked.

The detective shook his head. "Never met. I'm Bob Jones, with the Grand Springs Police Department. My partner will be in soon.'' He jerked his head toward the door. ''He's talking to the nurses right now.''

Trying to verify everything I'm telling him, Tom thought, surprising himself with his certainty. He filed the information away and focused on the detective.

Bob Jones stared at him for a moment, trying to intimidate him. Again, Tom wasn't sure how he knew it, but he did. Finally the detective said, ''So you don't remember anything that happened to you last night.''

''Detective, I don't remember anything at all, including my name. I'm taking it on faith that it's Tom Flynt.''

''That was the name on the driver's license we found with you,'' the detective said deliberately.

Tom frowned at him. ''Are you saying that it's a false driver's license?'' he asked after a moment.

''I'm not saying anything. I'm just stating a fact. And I'm the one asking the questions.'' He leaned closer. ''Do you remember Grand Springs?''

''Not at all. Do I live here?''

''Apparently not. The address on your driver's license is from Missouri. The St. Louis area. Does that ring a bell?''

Tom thought for a moment and almost shook his head until the stabbing pain reminded him not to. ''No. St. Louis sounds as unfamiliar as everything else.''

The detective nodded, as if that were what he'd expected Tom to say. He reached into his pocket and pulled out a small rectangle. ''This look familiar?''

He was holding a driver's license, and Tom could tell it was his. He remembered the face from the glimpse he'd gotten in the mirror earlier. Otherwise, it looked like a complete stranger. "No, it doesn't," he said quietly.

The detective reached into a bag and pulled out a huge, ugly handgun. "How about this?"

Tom heard Tina gasp beside him, but he didn't look up at her. "I don't remember that, either."

"The paramedics found it strapped to your back." He narrowed his eyes and gave Tom a hard look. "You didn't have a permit with you to carry concealed."

"I don't know what to say, Detective." Tom continued staring at the gun. "I honestly don't remember."

The detective stared at him for a few moments, then dropped the gun back into the bag. "We'll be holding on to this for the time being. Let me tell you what happened last night."

Tom managed to nod. He was beginning to get a really bad feeling from Detective Jones.

"There was a big masquerade ball here at the Grand Springs Empress Hotel last night. It was thrown by Jonathan Steele, CEO of Steele Enterprises. At this ball, Steele's half brother David and his wife Lisa were shot and killed. Two people ran out of the hotel and drove away. You were one of them. We found you by the side of the road, half an hour later. Your car had gone off the road and rolled over."

The detective gave him a hard look. "So you can see why we want to talk to you. We want to know who you are. And why you ran out of that ball."

"I'd like to know that myself." Tom held the detective's gaze, although his head throbbed with pain. "When I remember, you'll be the first to know."

Jones's hard, assessing gaze stayed on him for what felt like a long time, then he nodded. "I'll be back to talk to you later, when we get more information. In the meantime, don't think about leaving town."

Before Tom could answer, Tina stepped in front of him and faced Detective Jones. "I'm going to have to ask you to leave now, Detective," she said, and Tom heard the steel in her voice. "Mr. Flynt has a serious injury and I won't allow you to badger him."

A wave of gratitude welled up inside Tom, but he couldn't allow himself to look at Tina. He continued to watch the detective. "It's all right, Ms. White. Detective Jones can ask all the questions he wants."

"I'm through for now," Jones answered, but his stony gaze swept from Tom to Tina and back. "But I'll be back."

He turned and walked out of the room. When he was finally gone, Tina turned back to him. "How dare he imply that you're somehow connected to that murder?"

Tom shrugged. "He's looking at the evidence, and so far it would seem to support that. Apparently since I ran out of the ball after the shooting, that makes me a suspect in his eyes."

"No one, including you, knows why you ran out of that room," Tina said flatly. "I thought a person is innocent until proven guilty."

"He's just doing his job," Tom answered quietly.

Before Tina could respond, another man walked into the room. Rugged and broad shouldered, his gray eyes were just as penetrating as Detective Jones's. He glanced at Tina, then examined Tom thoroughly.

"Your partner just left." Tom couldn't have said why he thought this man was a police officer, but he was sure of it.

The blond man gave him a quick grin. "For a guy who's lost his memory, you're pretty good at identifying cops."

Tom shrugged uneasily, unsure of why he'd been so certain of the other man's occupation. "Just a guess."

"And a good one." The man came to a stop next to the bed and held out his hand. "Stone Richardson. I'm a detective with the Grand Springs Police Department. I'm working on the Steele murder case."

Tina waited for Tom to shake the detective's hand, then stepped closer to the bed, sliding between him and the detective. "Your colleague was just here," she said, crossing her arms in front of her chest. "He asked Mr. Flynt a number of questions, which he couldn't answer. There's no point in asking him again."

Stone Richardson held up his hands. "Whoa, I'm not here to ask Mr. Flynt the same questions. And I'm sorry if Bob upset you. I know he can come on a little too strong sometimes. That's just his style." He hesitated, then said, "The nurses said you seem to have a case of complete amnesia—you can't remember a thing. I wanted to talk to you to see if there was anything I could do to help."

"That's kind of you, Detective," Tom said slowly. "But I'm not sure what you could do, unless you recognize me."

Stone shook his head. "Never saw you before in my life. But your situation reminds me of a case I worked on in Grand Springs a few years ago. One of the witnesses in that case had amnesia, too.''

"Did he get his memory back?" Tom asked eagerly.

"Eventually."

"But it would help you with this case if I got my memory back a lot more quickly than eventually." Tom didn't take his eyes off the detective.

"Yes, but I know you can't push it. I just thought there might be something I could do."

"Thank you, Detective," Tom answered quietly, "but I'm not sure what that would be. I'll let you know as soon as I remember anything."

Stone nodded. "I'll stop by regularly and let you know if we find any new information." He turned to look at Tina. "And just for the record, I do believe he's innocent unless and until I prove him guilty."

He turned around and walked out the door before either of them could say anything. Finally Tom said, "Thank you, Ms. White."

"For what?"

"For defending me to Detectives Richardson and Jones. You have no idea if I'm guilty or not."

Her eyes flashed blue fire. "And neither do they. But Jones was assuming you were."

"You have to admit, if I did what they're saying I did, it looks pretty suspicious."

"There could have been a number of reasons you ran out of the hotel," Tina said hotly. "Maybe you're a police officer. Maybe you were trying to catch the killer."

"If I were a police officer here in Grand Springs, don't you think Jones and Richardson would know it?"

She looked away. "All right, maybe you're not a Grand Springs police officer. But that doesn't mean you're guilty of something."

"Why are you defending me like this, Ms. White?" he asked, his heart suddenly pounding. "You don't know me, either."

"Someone has to defend you." She looked at him again, and he could see the conviction in her eyes. "Until they find your family, there's no one else to speak for you."

"Thank you," he said, moved by her words. "That's very generous."

"You don't look like a criminal. And you don't act like one, either."

"What does a criminal look like?" Tom felt his mouth curving into a smile.

"Not like you," Tina answered immediately.

"I want to know the truth," he said. "Even if the truth is that I was involved in this crime. I want to know who I am, even if it means I'm a criminal."

"That's why I defended you." Tina bent closer, staring into his eyes. "A criminal wouldn't want that. A criminal would be trying to hide the truth. A criminal would be looking to shift the blame to someone else. Only a person with integrity would say that he wanted to know the truth, regardless of the circumstances."

Lost in the deep blue of Tina's eyes, Tom could almost believe she was speaking the truth. Almost. But he couldn't allow himself to believe it.

"It doesn't matter what the truth is. I want to know it," he said. "And if there is anything I can do to speed up the return of my memory, I'll do it."

"Dr. Wilson ordered a neurological exam," Tina

said. "The neurologist will probably stop by this afternoon. We should know more after she looks at you."

Tom shut his eyes, suddenly very tired. When he opened them a few moments later, Tina was still standing above him, watching him with a worried look on her face.

"What's wrong?" he asked.

"I shouldn't have let those two detectives talk to you," she said, a frown furrowing her forehead. "They tired you out."

"It's okay," he said. "They have a job to do. And I want to find out who I am as quickly as possible."

She nodded, but there was a militant look in her eyes. "They won't bother you again today."

"Are you going to stand guard at the door to my room?" he teased.

She gave him an answering grin. "I won't have to. We took a class in nursing school about this kind of situation. It was called Withering Looks and Stern Frowns. Guaranteed to get rid of any unwanted visitors."

"Sounds great." The pain in his head and his side was pulling him down into a spiral of darkness. He forced himself to keep his eyes open for another moment. "I'll count on you to keep the dragons away."

She smoothed the sheet over his chest, then lightly touched his hand. "I'm working on this floor, so I'll check on you frequently."

He wanted to call her back, to ask her to touch him again. But the darkness was pulling too hard, tugging him into the void. Tom watched her walk out the door, noticing her long, slender body and the gentle sway of her hips. He held onto the image as he slid into sleep.

Tina stood at the desk in the hallway, checking on some patient records, when a blond woman stepped out of Tom's room and slid her hands into the pockets of her white jacket. When she reached the desk, she said, "Can I have Tom Flynt's chart?"

"What do you think, Dr. Mellon?" Tina asked.

"He definitely has amnesia," the neurologist answered. "He seems to be completely blocked."

"What's his prognosis?"

"Good, I'd say. But I have no idea how long it will last. At least he doesn't have any other neurological problems. His brain scan was normal and all the tests I gave him were normal."

"Treatment?"

The neurologist smiled. "Tincture of time. His memories will eventually come back. But someone is going to have to spend a lot of time with him, talking to him. Are you the nurse who's taking care of him?"

Tina nodded.

"Spend as much time as you can with him," the doctor said. She made a few notations on Tom's chart, then walked away.

"Well, Tina, it looks like you're going to have your hands full with that patient," one of the nurses said.

Tina nodded. But her heart sped up in her chest at the prospect of spending time with Tom Flynt.

Chapter 3

Although Tina checked on him frequently, Tom spent most of the rest of the day sleeping. It was perfectly normal, she knew, and was the best treatment for his injuries, but she couldn't control her disappointment every time she opened his door and saw his eyes closed.

"I'm just dopey from the lack of sleep," she muttered to herself as she closed his door for the last time at the end of her shift. But whatever the reason, she was absurdly disappointed that she hadn't gotten the chance to say goodbye to her patient.

She walked more slowly than usual to the nursing desk and picked up her purse and her jacket. The supervisor looked up at her.

"Are you on tomorrow, Tina?"

She nodded. "I'll be here for the afternoon shift..." she hesitated, then added "...unless you need me earlier."

The supervisor gave her a sharp look, then shook her head. "Don't go volunteering like that, Tina. Someone might take you up on the offer."

"I'm not doing anything important tomorrow. Do you need an extra pair of hands?" she asked eagerly.

"I don't think so." She looked at Tina questioningly. "You were here late last night, weren't you?"

When Tina nodded, the other woman scowled. "Go home and get some sleep, White. And don't come back until tomorrow afternoon."

Tina headed for the elevator, resisting the impulse to look back toward Tom Flynt's room. He was in good hands, she told herself. And she did need to get some sleep tonight.

But she was back at the hospital the next day several hours before her shift began. She said hello to the nurses clustered around the desk, then slipped into Tom Flynt's room. She merely wanted to see if he had regained any of his memory, she told herself.

He was sitting up in bed, reading a newspaper. When he saw her walk in the door, he put it down and gave her a smile. Her stomach swooped toward her toes.

"Good morning," he said, his eyes warming as they rested on her. "I wondered where you were, Ms. White."

"Please, call me Tina," she said. "We're going to be spending a lot of time together."

"Tina." He seemed to savor the sound of her name, and a shiver of pleasure rippled through her. "That will be something to look forward to." She couldn't miss the flare of pleasure in his eyes, and warmth blossomed inside her.

"How are you feeling this morning?" She struggled to ignore her body's reaction and get back on safer ground.

"Other than the fact that I have no idea who I am or what I'm supposed to be doing in Grand Springs, I feel pretty good."

She picked up the chart at the end of his bed and realized that it was time for one of the nurses to listen to his chest and check his wound. "Let me take a look at you."

Her fingers moved gently over the bandage on his head, easing the tape away from his skin. She nodded as she looked at the wound. "Your head is healing nicely," she said. "No problems here."

Then she took her stethoscope out of her pocket and placed it on his chest. She told herself to ignore the warmth of his skin and the vitality that seemed to shimmer in the air around him. He was a patient, she told herself. Nothing more.

Finally, she stepped back and folded the stethoscope back into her pocket. She noticed that her hands were shaking and she shoved them into her pockets, too. "Sounds good. I don't think there's been any more bleeding into your chest, but Dr. Wilson will probably want to get another scan in a day or two, just to be sure."

He sat in the bed, watching her, a bemused expression on his face. "What time does your shift usually start, Tina?"

The sound of her name on his lips made her tingle with pleasure, but she held his gaze. "Three o'clock. But because of what happened at the Steele ball, there are a lot of extra patients right now, so I thought I'd come in early to help out."

"I'm glad," he said, watching her. "I missed you."

Her heart leaped in her chest, and she wanted to tell him that she'd missed him, too. Instead she said, "You feel comfortable with me because you remember my voice. It's the only thing that's at all familiar to you." She gave him a bright smile. "But that's okay, because you're going to be seeing a lot of me in the next few days."

He leaned back against the pillows on the bed, but he didn't take his eyes off her. She thought she saw a flash of pleasure, quickly hidden, but she couldn't be sure. She didn't have a lot of experience with men, other than as patients.

"It seems I spent most of yesterday sleeping," he said, watching her.

She scowled. "I should never have let those detectives grill you like they did. They tired you out."

To her surprise, he laughed. "No one's ever been so protective toward me. I think I like it," he said. His smile slowly faded, and she saw a hint of fear in his eyes. "How did I remember that when I can't even remember my own name?"

"Don't worry." She couldn't stop herself from touching his arm. "That's how your memory comes back, in bits and pieces. You'll remember something and have no idea what it means, but gradually you'll get more and more pieces of the puzzle, and pretty soon you'll remember everything."

He stared up at her. "You're very reassuring, Tina," he said, his voice quiet. "Are you just saying that to make me feel better?"

"Of course not. Lying to you isn't going to help you." She sat down on the chair next to his bed. "I have to admit, Mr. Flynt, that I haven't taken care of many patients with amnesia. But I looked it up in my nursing books last night.'' She swallowed as she remembered her determined search for every bit of information she could find. ''And that's what all the books said. You generally regain your memory in bits and pieces.''

''Please, call me Tom,'' he said. He gave her a smile that looked forced. ''It may not sound familiar, but apparently it's what I'm supposed to be called. And it sounds a lot better than Mr. Flynt.''

''All right...Tom.'' Her voice sounded different, low and intimate in the quiet of the room.

She sounded like a woman talking to her lover.

Tina swallowed and clenched her hands tightly in her lap. What was she doing? What was the matter with her? She couldn't possibly be attracted to this man. He was a complete stranger to her. And for all of the kindness in his eyes, there was an aura of danger around him. For heaven's sake, he even carried a gun.

She thought she had learned her lesson well, all those years ago.

''Are you as conscientious with all your patients?'' Tom asked, and she gave herself a mental shake.

''What do you mean?''

''You said you went home and read up on amnesia. Do you do that whenever you have an unusual patient?''

''Of course,'' she said immediately, grateful for the change of subject. ''If I don't know what to do for a patient, how can I take care of him or her properly?''

''Ouch,'' he said, but there was a twinkle in his eyes. ''I thought I was special.''

"You are," she said, giving him a grin. It was far easier to maintain her distance if she was bantering with him. "Right now, you're my favorite patient. Since you don't remember anything, I can tell you whatever I want and you'll believe me. That's exactly the kind of patient I like."

"I promise to be very gullible," he said solemnly.

She laughed and stood up. "And if I believe that, you have some oceanfront property just outside of town you'd like to sell me, right?"

"You've got it." The smile lingered in his eyes as he watched her. "What's on the agenda for today, Tina?"

"Rest," she said firmly. "You have to take it easy so your lung can heal."

"I was figuring to go out and get in a few miles of hard running," he said, then stopped. Tina recognized the startled expression on his face.

"You've remembered that you like to run," she said.

"Yes." He stared at her. "I don't know how I remembered, but I do."

"That's another piece to the puzzle," she said. "And that's what the textbooks I read last night said would happen. You'd remember when you weren't trying to force it."

"It's going to be hard not to."

"I know." Tina felt a wave of sympathy for him. She wasn't sure how she would feel in Tom's circumstances, but she knew she would try as hard as possible to get her memories back. Even the bad ones. "I'll try to keep you distracted."

"You won't have to work very hard at that."

This time she couldn't mistake the heat in his eyes,

or the message there. To her surprise, she felt an answering warmth bloom inside her. She stared at him for a moment, shocked, then hurriedly turned away.

"Does that mean you're easily entertained?" Her voice sounded strained, and she struggled to even it out.

"It means I'm going to selfishly hog as much of your time and attention as I can."

She didn't have to be looking at Tom to know what he meant. The tone of his voice told her he was interested. She hoped to find the words to tell him to save his breath, that she wasn't interested in getting involved with him or anyone else, but they wouldn't come. Finally she turned around to face him.

"You're my patient," she said, trying to make her voice firm. "I'll give you as much time as you need." She hoped that he saw only professional interest in her face.

The gleam of satisfaction that filled his eyes told her that she hadn't succeeded. But he nodded slowly. "That's fair," he said. "I know you have other patients."

"And I have to start taking care of them," she said. "Or my supervisor will have my head."

"I don't want to be blamed for the loss of that beautiful hair and those gorgeous eyes," he said. "Go ahead. I'm not going anywhere."

Tina nodded, not trusting herself to say anything more. She murmured something incoherent and practically ran through the door. She paused when she was in the hall, taking deep breaths to calm herself.

"Are you okay, Tina?" one of her fellow nurses asked, a worried expression on her face. "You look kind of dazed."

"I'm fine." She forced a smile. "Lack of sleep, I guess."

The other nurse rolled her eyes. "Tell me about it. This place has been a madhouse for the last thirty-six hours."

She hurried off, and Tina stood in the hallway for a few moments, composing herself. Then she tried to put her reaction to Tom firmly out of her head. She walked over to the desk and studied the board where their assignments were posted. "Who else am I taking care of today?"

Tom watched the door close behind Tina with a final-sounding click. He heard her speaking to someone in the hallway, then listened as her footsteps receded down the hall. She was gone, but she'd be back. For the first time, he found something positive about his dilemma.

Right woman, wrong time, he told himself bitterly. He had no right to be interested in Tina White. He knew nothing about himself, not even his name. He could be married with ten children, for all he knew.

He looked down and studied his ring finger on his left hand. There was no wedding ring, and no pale line like he'd recently removed one. He had been telling her the truth yesterday. He didn't feel married.

But that didn't change anything. Although he was attracted to her, found her interesting and sexy, he had no right to pursue that attraction. And for all he knew, she could be married herself. Or at least involved with someone.

But she didn't seem involved, either. There was a remote quality about Tina, an innocence that surrounded her. He'd noticed her reaction when she realized he was attracted to her. He didn't think the shock he'd seen in her eyes had been faked.

Could he do the right thing? Could he submerge his interest in Tina, bury it deep enough that it would wither and die? He hoped so. He didn't want to cause her any pain.

But he would be in the hospital for a few more days, so he would enjoy the time he could spend with her. She had told him not to force his memory to return. Thinking about Tina would be a pleasant alternative to wondering who he was.

He listened carefully, but he couldn't hear her in the hallway. She wouldn't be back for a while, he suspected. She had practically run out of his room, and she would busy herself with other patients for a while.

He wasn't sure how he knew that, but he was certain he was right. The irony of it put a grim smile on his mouth. He didn't know his own name, but he knew Tina well enough after two days to predict how she would act.

He looked away from the door and clicked on the television set suspended above the foot of his bed. Maybe if he listened to the news, it would shake something loose in his brain.

A couple of hours later he had almost fallen asleep when the door opened a crack. He glanced over at the door and felt his pulse accelerate when he saw Tina in the doorway.

"I thought you were sleeping," she said.

"Only bored," he said. He turned off the television. "Even CNN gets boring after a while."

She stopped next to his bed. "You knew about CNN?"

"It appears so. I guess I'm fine at bringing up some details, but not the important ones."

She smiled at him, but he could see the careful distance in her eyes. "It will come," she said. "Give it some time. It's been less than forty-eight hours."

"I thought about that, and I have an idea. If I went back to the scene of the accident, maybe the scene of the ball I was at, it might jog some memories loose. What do you think?"

She nodded slowly. "Maybe it would. You'll have to try that when you're back on your feet."

He scowled. "I was thinking about today."

For a moment she stared at him, then laughed. For the first time since she'd come back into his room, she relaxed. "Right. You have a concussion and an abraded lung, and you think we're going to let you go running around Grand Springs?"

"I wouldn't run. I would drive."

Her smile faded. "You're serious, aren't you?"

"Of course I'm serious. I want to find out who I am and what I was doing that night."

She sank down onto the chair next to his bed and put her hand on top of his. He wanted to turn his hand over and twine his fingers with hers, to press their palms together, but he didn't dare. Instead, he savored the feel of her warm hand and tried to hide his sudden rush of desire.

"Tom, the detectives who were here yesterday are doing their best to find your family. There's nothing more you can do right now."

"I could look for myself. Maybe I'd remember."

He leaned forward, ignoring the pain in his side. Shifting his hand, he gripped her fingers while he searched the depths of her blue eyes. "I have to know, Tina."

Something flickered deep within her eyes. It was a spark of excitement, an answering urgency. She understood, and she wanted to let him go. Tom tightened his hand on hers, and waited for her to agree.

Then she shook her head. "No way, Flynt. You're not getting out of this bed until tomorrow, and then the farthest you're going is to the bathroom." She eased her hand away from his and stood up. "You can prowl around Grand Springs all you want when you're released. But for now, I'm afraid you're stuck with CNN and me."

He studied her face, saw the shadow of awareness in her eyes, and leaned back against the pillow. For a moment, she'd been tempted. And she wanted to go with him. For now, it was enough.

"If I can't leave, then you and CNN sound like a pretty good deal," he said, trying to keep his voice light. "But admit it, you were tempted."

To his surprise, instead of teasing him back, something that looked close to panic flared in her eyes. Then it was gone, and the remote professional was back. "I was tempted to smack you." She gave him a stern look. "Your injuries could have been life threatening. You are incredibly lucky to get away as lightly as you have. So instead of trying to get out of the hospital way before you're ready, you should be thanking God for your luck."

"You wanted to take me, didn't you, Tina?" He didn't know what demon taunted him to press the issue.

"I wanted no such thing," she said primly, but her eyes told the truth. She *had* been tempted.

"Tell me, Tina, do you ever break the rules?"

"No." Her answer was much too quick and much too final, and he saw a shadow of pain in her eyes. She had broken the rules at least once in her life. To his surprise, jealousy flashed through him as he wondered if the broken rules involved a man.

He settled back against the pillows, but he didn't take his eyes off her. "We'll have to work on that."

He half expected her to turn around and run out of the room, but she surprised him again. Tilting her head to the side, she watched him as a small smile curled her lips. "I was right. You are a dangerous man."

"What do you mean?"

"You like to break the rules. You want to play the game your own way."

"Maybe I do," he said slowly, turning the idea over in his mind. It felt right. "But that doesn't mean I'm dangerous."

Regret flared in Tina's eyes. "You are to someone who follows the rules," she said quietly. "And I always follow the rules."

"Always, Tina?"

She held his gaze for a few moments, then looked away. "Whenever it counts."

He couldn't read the expression on her face, the emotions in her eyes. But he knew that there was far more to Tina White than showed on the surface. He wasn't the only one in the room with secrets.

"A little rule-breaking is good for the soul," he said lightly. "We'll have to work on that."

With an effort, she gave him a smile. "You can work on it all you want when you get out of here. While you're my patient, you follow my rules."

"Gladly." He grinned up at her. "Just tell me what you want."

This time her smile was genuine. "I want you to get better and regain your memory. And driving around Grand Springs isn't the way it's going to happen."

"Since you probably hid all of my clothes, I guess I don't have any choice," he said, and was rewarded with a low, throaty chuckle.

"You could always leave in your hospital gown," she teased. "Of course, it might get kind of breezy."

"No, thanks." He reached around to make sure his gown was tucked in. "I guess I'll wait."

"I knew you'd see it my way." She turned to walk out of the room, and he searched desperately for a way to keep her with him for a few more minutes.

"Tina, wait."

She spun around. "Is something wrong?"

"I just wanted to ask you a question." He hesitated, not sure how to get the information he wanted. Finally he said, "It's really good of you to come in early to take care of me. I appreciate it. But isn't your family getting upset that you're spending all your time at the hospital?"

She watched him for a moment, and once again he saw a shadow of pain in her eyes. "First of all, I'm not coming in early just for you. There are a lot more patients than usual."

But he saw the truth in her eyes, and his heart leaped. She *was* coming in early just for him.

"And you don't have to worry about what my family thinks. I live by myself. My free time is my own."

"I didn't mean to pry."

"It's all right. I'm not offended." She gave him a

strained smile. "I'll be back in a while. Some of those other patients need care, too."

He listened to her footsteps recede down the hall as he closed his eyes. Damned if she wasn't right. He was in no shape to go jaunting off around Grand Springs. He could barely carry on a conversation without getting tired out.

But he had gotten the information he wanted, he thought, exultant. Tina wasn't involved with anyone. He was sure of it. If she had been, she wouldn't have been so casual about living by herself.

Unexpected hunger stirred inside him. If Tina was his woman, he thought, he wouldn't want to let her out of his sight. If he was involved with Tina, she wouldn't have any free time. He'd want to spend every second of it with her.

If Tina was his lover, he'd make sure everyone in the world knew it.

Chapter 4

Ten hours later, Tina leaned against the desk, weariness threatening to overwhelm her. Two days without enough sleep were catching up to her. It was time to go home and fall into bed.

And she wouldn't check on Tom again, she told herself firmly. He was probably asleep, and if he wasn't, he should be.

As she was gathering her jacket and purse to leave, a voice behind her said, "Ms. White?"

She turned around to see Detective Bob Jones standing at the nursing desk. Her breath caught in a quick gasp of fear. He wouldn't be here so late if it wasn't serious. Swallowing once, she said, "Hello, Detective. What can I do for you?"

He watched her for a moment, and she felt as if he could see all the way inside her head, see the fear she'd tried to hide. Finally, he said, "I need to see Tom Flynt."

"At this time of night? I'm sure he's asleep."

"I have some questions that can't wait."

"He's not going anywhere, Detective. He'll still be here in the morning."

He narrowed his eyes. "I don't need your permission to talk to him, Ms. White. He's a suspect in a major crime, and I need him to clear some things up for me. Now do you want to wake him up for me, or should I do it myself?"

"I'll wake him up." Shakily she turned away and walked down the hall. My God, what had they found out? This was the first time the detective had actually called Tom a suspect.

When she peered into Tom's room, she saw that he was sleeping. Slipping into the gloom of the darkened room, she motioned to the detective to wait outside.

She stood next to the bed for a moment, watching Tom breathe. His face was relaxed and his eyes were closed. At least he was free from the anxiety that she knew filled him whenever he was awake. She hated to wake him, hated to disturb him, but she knew she didn't have a choice.

"Tom, wake up," she whispered.

He didn't move. She touched his arm, once again trying to ignore the solid feel of him, the warmth that pulsed from him. "Tom, Detective Jones is here to talk to you."

His eyes fluttered open and he looked right at her. His mouth curved up in a smile and his hand reached for hers. "Tina," he said in a sleepy voice, "why are you still here?"

For a moment she returned the pressure of his hand, allowed herself to enjoy the warmth of his fingers curved around hers, then she gently slipped her hand away. "I was just leaving. I told Detective Jones to come back tomorrow, but he seems to think it's urgent."

The sleepy, satisfied look disappeared and Tom's eyes became more focused. He lifted himself in the bed, then pressed the button that would raise him up. He moved more easily than he had even that morning, but Tina could see that he was still uncomfortable.

"Do you want me to stay here while the detective talks to you?"

Tom looked over at her and smiled. "So you can protect me?"

"I want to make sure he doesn't tire you out."

"I want to talk to him, Tina, but I'd love for you to stay."

Tina turned around and nodded to Detective Jones, who stood in the doorway. He probably wanted to make sure I wasn't trying to help Tom escape through the window, she thought sourly. "You can come in now, Detective."

He walked up to the bed and stood looking down at Tom. Tina offered him the chair, but he ignored her. Finally he said, "We traced your driver's license, Flynt. It was a forgery."

Tina heard a gasp, and realized it had come from her. There was silence in the room. Finally, Tom said, "What is that supposed to mean?"

"It means that Missouri has no record of issuing a driver's license to you, ever. That license of yours was a fake, and a damned skillful one."

Tom studied the detective's face. He said, "And what else? I know there's more. I can see it in your face."

"For someone who says he's lost his memory, you seem to know quite a bit."

Tom shrugged. "I can't help what I remember or know."

"That's convenient."

"That's the way it is."

The two men stared at one another for another moment. The detective looked away first. He glanced down at the small notebook in his hand. "Your credit card bills are sent to a P.O. box in Missouri, too. The address that the post office has for the box doesn't exist. It's a vacant lot in a rough part of St. Louis." He rattled off an address to Tom, then looked at him. "Does that ring a bell?"

"Not at all."

The detective snapped the notebook shut and slipped it into his back pocket. "You've got a problem, Flynt..." he paused "...if that's really your name."

"It's the name on my credit cards and driver's license, isn't it?"

"That doesn't mean squat."

Tom shrugged, but Tina could see the tension in the line of his shoulders. "I'm sorry, Detective, but I can't give you any answers. The only reason I know my name is Tom Flynt is because you told me so."

"As far as I'm concerned, Flynt, you're a suspect in the murders of David and Lisa Steele." Detective Jones fixed his hard stare on Tom. "I'm going to do my best to get all the facts in this case. And when I do, I'm going to arrest you."

"There were a lot of people at this ball, weren't there?" Tom asked.

"Only a couple hundred of them," the detective shot back.

"Did any of them see me shoot the Steeles?"

"No." The admission was grudging. "No one saw the actual shooting. But several people saw you and another man running out of the ballroom immediately after the shooting. When I put that together with your fake identification and the gun we found with you, I add up two and two and get four. If you weren't the shooter, then I figure you for an accessory to the murders."

Tom stared at the detective, and Tina could see him trying to force himself to remember. She stepped forward to tell the detective to leave, but Tom grabbed her hand.

"Wait," he said without looking at her.

"What about my gun? Was it the murder weapon?" he asked the detective.

"We're checking that. And we'll need a set of fingerprints from you to run through the computer."

"Then all your evidence is circumstantial," Tom said slowly. "It wouldn't hold up in a court of law."

Detective Jones snorted. "Would this be called selective amnesia? For someone who claims they can't remember anything, you sure sound like you know what you're talking about."

Tom leaned back against the pillows, weariness etched on his face. "I told you, Detective, I can't help what I can remember. And I don't know why I know that. I just do."

"And I know this—" Detective Jones leaned closer to Tom "—don't plan on leaving town once you get out of the hospital, Mr. Flynt." There was a subtle emphasis on Tom's name. "We may not have any direct evidence yet, but I'll find it. And then I'll nail you.''

"You're welcome to try," Tom shot back. "I want to know the truth as much as you do."

The detective straightened. "We'll see if you're singing the same tune in a few days."

"In a few days, I hope I'll have regained my memory and I'll be able to tell you everything you want to know," Tom said coolly.

"I'm looking forward to it."

The detective nodded once at Tom, his eyes hard and suspicious, then turned and walked out of the room. Tina waited until his footsteps had faded away, then she dropped down onto the chair next to Tom's bed.

"He called you a suspect," she whispered, appalled.

"He more than suspects. He's certain," Tom answered bluntly.

"How can he act that way?" she cried. "What happened to 'innocent until proven guilty'?"

"He's a cop, Tina," Tom said, his voice weary. "He's going with what he has. And I look damned guilty."

"How can you say that?"

"My driver's license is phony, and the only address they have for me is a vacant lot in St. Louis. Plus I was carrying a gun. If I were a cop, I'd be just as suspicious."

"I'm sure there's a reasonable explanation." Her voice sounded desperate.

Tom finally smiled. "Thank you," he said, and he reached out and took her hand. "Thank you for taking my side. But I have to face the facts. Maybe I did have something to do with those people's deaths.''

"You didn't," she said automatically. "You're not a killer. You can't be."

Tom looked at Tina then, and for just a moment she saw his fear. Then it was gone, replaced by a warmth that made her breathless. "Your belief in me means more than I can tell you. But I won't know if I had anything to do with the murders until I get my memory back."

"You'll remember," she said, and heard the fierceness in her voice. "Then Detective Jones will have to look somewhere else."

Tom twined his fingers with hers and brought her hand to his mouth. "Thank you." His voice was hushed in the still, dark room. "I hope I don't disappoint you when we know the truth."

"You won't." Tina studied Tom's face, unable to see even a hint of guilt or evil there. He wasn't a killer. She was sure of it. And if that made her a fool, she didn't care.

He brushed his lips against the back of her hand, then turned her hand over and pressed a kiss into her palm. Blood thickened in her veins and her heart began to pound as his lips lingered. Her skin felt scorched where he'd touched her. She felt her hand tremble, and felt Tom's hand shaking, too.

"You need to go home and get some sleep," he said. But he didn't let her hand go, and she didn't pull away. It was late at night, and her common sense and natural caution had vanished. She didn't care about sleeping. She didn't care that she had to be back at work early the next afternoon. All she wanted to do was sit in this room with Tom, holding his hand.

"Tina," he whispered, turning toward her.

"What?" She stared at him, unable to breathe, unable to move.

He was inches away from her when he stopped suddenly, then leaned back against the pillows. He gently disengaged his hand from hers, then curled his hand into a fist and closed his eyes. "Go home."

"I'm not ready to go home."

Tom opened his eyes and looked at her. "Yes, you are. Go home, Tina. Get some sleep. And don't have too much faith in me. I don't want to disappoint you."

"You won't," she whispered.

"That remains to be seen." He opened his eyes after a moment and managed to smile. "I'll see you tomorrow."

Slowly, she stood up. "I'll be in early."

His smile deepened, extended to his eyes. "I know. I'll be looking forward to it."

She resisted the impulse to bend down and kiss him, shocking herself with the thought. "Good night," she said quickly, then hurried from the room. She paused in the hallway, took a deep breath, then walked quickly back to the nurses' station and grabbed her belongings. She didn't even notice the cool air hitting her overheated face as she rushed to her car. She needed to be back in her own home, where she belonged. She needed to be grounded, to remember what couldn't be. And there was no place better for that than her home, the house she'd lived in for her whole life. If she needed any reminders about getting involved with a man, all she had to do was look around her house and remember.

* * *

Tom forced himself to be patient for the next day, and the day after that. But no more memories returned, in spite of the odd little flashes of knowledge he had. It was all there, he knew. But it was hidden behind a veil, and no amount of struggling allowed him to rip that veil aside. His past, his identity, were still in limbo.

The only reality in his life was Tina, and she was becoming far too important to him. He hardly slept at all the night after Detective Jones's visit, and it wasn't because of the detective's accusations. It was because he had almost kissed Tina.

He spent half his time cursing himself for allowing the attraction between them to flame out of control, and half his time regretting that he had stopped before he kissed her.

Tina breezed into his room late in the afternoon of his fourth day in the hospital. "The nurses said the neurologist was in to see you this morning. She hasn't written her notes in the chart yet. What did she have to say?"

"That nothing had changed. It was a big surprise to me," he said sourly.

Tina sat down in the chair next to his bed. "You're doing fine. You're remembering more every day."

"I remembered that I like the Chicago Cubs. Now that's a real breakthrough."

Tina laughed. "It tells me what kind of person you are."

"And what kind is that? Terminally stupid?"

"Of course not. You're loyal, and an optimist, and an incurable romantic."

He laughed in spite of himself. Tina could always cheer him up when he was feeling sorry for himself.

"I guess that's one way to describe a Cubs fan." His smile faded. "Maybe it means I'm originally from the Chicago area."

"Did you call Detective Jones and tell him?"

Tom shook his head. "Not yet. But I should."

"Why don't you contact that other detective who was working with Jones? I think his name was Richardson. He seemed a lot more sympathetic. At least he acted like he believed you have amnesia."

"Maybe I will. It wouldn't hurt to check the Chicago area."

"Would you like me to call him for you and ask him to stop by?"

"Thanks, but I'll do it. I want to hear his voice when I talk to him."

"Why is that?"

"I don't know." Tom paused with his hand on the phone. "I have no idea. But I know it's important that I listen to him."

"Go ahead, then." She reached for the phone book that was in the room, and found the correct number. "Here you go."

Tom's heart pounded as he listened to the phone ring. "Grand Springs Police Station," a bored voice finally said. Tom asked for Detective Stone Richardson, and listened to the clicks as he was connected.

"Richardson here."

"Detective, this is Tom Flynt. I've remembered a small detail that might not help your investigation, but might help you find out who I am."

"Great. I was going to come see you anyway. Can I come over right now?" Richardson asked immediately.

"Thank you. I would appreciate that." Tom hung

up the phone and turned to Tina. "He's coming right over."

"Great." Tina gave him a warm smile, and he wanted to reach for her. He'd wanted to reach for her every time he'd seen her since that night in his room. But just like every other time, he resisted.

She had been more distant since that night, too. It was for the best, he told himself. Until he knew who and what he was, he had no business getting involved with Tina.

"Dr. Wilson said you're doing so well that he might consider releasing you tomorrow," she said.

"Yeah, he told me the same thing. Maybe then I can take a look at some of the places around town. It might jog my memory."

"Just because you're leaving the hospital doesn't mean you're completely back to normal," she warned. "You're going to have to take it easy for a while."

"Doc Wilson said I have the hardest head of any patient he's ever seen."

"And I'm sure he meant it figuratively as well as literally," she said scowling.

Tom grinned to himself. Tina was so protective that he knew just what buttons to push to get her going.

"That doesn't mean you can go running around Grand Springs tomorrow."

He allowed the smile to creep onto his face. "I know. But it's so much fun to tease you."

Tina shook her head as she laughed and stood up. "I should know better by now, shouldn't I?" Her smile faded a little. "Do you know where you'll stay?"

"In a hotel, I suppose." He kept the smile on his

face, although it felt forced. "I guess my credit cards are still good, even though they're registered to a phony address. Apparently they're still being paid."

"I checked with the emergency room for you. They didn't find a hotel key that night. But there was so much confusion it probably got thrown away. Maybe the police will have figured out where you were staying," she said.

"Maybe so." He didn't think so. If he had, Detective Jones would have let him know, especially if they'd found anything incriminating.

"We won't let you leave without having a place for you to stay," Tina said firmly. "I'll look for a hotel for you myself, if I have to."

"I can't let you do that."

"You can't stop me, either." She grinned at him, then turned to go. "My other patients are probably wondering where I am. I'll see you later."

She was almost at the door when he said, "Tina?"

She turned around immediately. "Yes?"

"Will you come by when Detective Richardson gets here? I'd like you to be here when I talk to him."

"Of course. I'll keep an eye open for him."

Twenty minutes later, Tina stuck her head into the room. "Tom?" she called.

"Is Richardson here?" he asked.

"Yes. Do you want me to send him in?"

"Please."

Tina turned and spoke to someone behind her in the hall, then Stone Richardson walked in. Tina followed him and closed the door.

"I have some news for you, Flynt," Stone said. "We found out where you were staying."

Tom's heart began to pound. "Where?"

"In an extended-stay hotel on the outskirts of town. It's one of those places that cater to business travelers who need to stay in a town more than a few days. It's more like a small apartment than a hotel—it has a bedroom and a kitchen and a living room." He grinned at Tom. "All the comforts of home."

"How did you find it?"

"I went to all the hotels in town to see if you were registered."

Tom tightened his hands on the rail next to his bed. "And was I registered as Tom Flynt?"

"You were. The clerk even recognized your picture."

"Could he tell you anything else?"

"Only that you said you were from St. Louis."

Tom's heart began to pound. "What address did I give them?"

Stone watched him carefully. "The same address that's on your P.O. box."

"You mean the vacant lot."

"Yes."

"I suppose you got a search warrant and went through the room?"

"We did. Jones was very thorough. But he didn't find a thing." Stone's gray eyes bored into him. "And how did you know we would have to get a search warrant?"

Tom shrugged. "Too much television, I guess." But the question had shaken him. He had known instinctively that the police would need a search warrant to go through his belongings. How had he known that? Was it because he was a criminal and had been served with search warrants in the past? He'd like to think it was because he was involved in law enforcement, but that seemed unlikely. Surely the Grand Springs police would have known.

"What did you want to tell me?" Stone's voice interrupted his thoughts and jerked him back to the present.

"I wanted to tell you that I remembered that I'm a Chicago Cubs baseball fan."

"You have my sympathy," Richardson said immediately, grinning.

Tom's answering smile was reluctant. "So I gather. But I thought it might help to locate my family."

The detective's smile faded. "I'll start looking in the Chicago area. But it might not lead to anything," he warned. "Maybe you only lived there for a few years and moved on."

"I know. But it's better than nothing."

The detective regarded him with sympathy. "You'll figure it out. Your memory will all come back."

"Tell me, Richardson, do you think I'm involved with those murders?"

"Absolutely." Stone answered without hesitation. "You're connected to them somehow. But until I know exactly how, I'm reserving judgment."

"Your partner hasn't done that."

"Bob sees things in black and white. It's a useful viewpoint for a cop, but I prefer shades of gray."

Tom nodded. It was the best he could expect, and he respected the other man for his honesty. "Thanks, Detective."

"Don't mention it. I'll start working on a possible Chicago connection." He glanced over at Tina, then back at Tom. "The doc says you might be getting out of the hospital tomorrow. Keep us posted. And don't leave Grand Springs."

"Don't worry. Until I remember who I am, I don't have anyplace to go."

"Right." Richardson nodded to Tina, then to him, and left the room.

"Well, at least you know where you'll be going when you leave," Tina said brightly. "And maybe looking at your belongings will jog your memory."

"I hope so," he said quietly.

Before Tina could answer, the door to the room opened and Dr. Wilson walked in. "Hi, Tina. Tom."

Tina nodded to him, and Tom thought he saw a whisper of regret on her face. She stared at the doctor as if she were bracing herself for something.

"I've got good news. I've written your release," the doctor said to Tom. "You can leave the hospital tomorrow."

Tina's shoulders slumped, and Tom's heart pounded. Tina was sorry he was leaving! She didn't want him to go.

"That's great news," he heard her say, and when he looked over at her, he saw a forced cheerfulness in her face.

"It's wonderful," he said dutifully, but he was disappointed. He was going to miss Tina.

"I'll have instructions for you before you leave, and I'll want to see you frequently, but your lung has healed and your head injury is no longer life-threatening. There's no reason you have to stay here."

Tom nodded. "Thank you."

Tina gripped the bed rail, and Tom saw her knuckles turn white. "I'll go get the paperwork started. You probably want to talk to Dr. Wilson.'' She turned and hurried out of the room, letting the door close firmly behind her.

Tom watched her go. He missed her already.

But he didn't have to miss Tina. There was no reason he couldn't keep on seeing her after he was out of the hospital. His heart lightened until he remembered one very good reason. He didn't have a thing to offer her. Not even his real name.

Chapter 5

Tina maneuvered her car to the curb and watched the orderly push Tom's wheelchair over to the passenger door. Then the young man opened the door and helped Tom slide onto the seat.

Tina's heart fluttered as the orderly shut the door and Tom looked at her. "Thank you," he said quietly. "Taking me to my hotel goes above and beyond the call of duty."

"Don't mention it," she said, her breath fluttery and her hands sweating on the steering wheel. "It's on my way home anyway."

"But this is your day off. You didn't even have to come to the hospital."

"Do you think I would have let my favorite patient leave without saying goodbye?" She tried to keep her voice light and teasing, and had a feeling she failed miserably.

"You could have said goodbye yesterday."

"All right, I'll admit it. I'm a sucker for men who can't remember anything." She glanced over at him and tried to give him a bright smile. "It makes it so much easier to tell them what to do."

She kept her eyes on the road in front of her, but she could feel Tom's eyes on her. "You can tell me what to do any time," he said, his voice low and intimate in the cocoon of the car.

"Be careful," she warned. "I might take you up on that."

"Be my guest."

It was time to change the subject, she thought, her heart thumping. "Does anything look familiar?" she asked as they drove through the town of Grand Springs.

Out of the corner of her eye she saw him glance out the window. "I haven't been paying attention."

"I thought you couldn't wait to get out of the hospital and look around?"

"I was distracted."

"Oh." Her skin burned where his gaze touched her, and she swallowed hard. "Well, look around now."

"Yes, ma'am. Is this what you mean about being able to tell me what to do?"

"This is exactly what I mean."

Finally he looked away and stared out the window. "Is this the downtown area?" he asked.

"Yes, it is." She was so relieved to be talking about an impersonal subject that she talked too fast. "The hospital is on one side of town, and your hotel and my house are on the other side."

"Where was the ball?"

"On the same side of town as the hospital."

"Can we drive past the building where it was held?"

"Not now," she said firmly. "We can look at the hotel where the ball was held anytime. Right now you need to get to your apartment so you can take it easy."

"That's all I've been doing for the last five days," he protested. "I don't need to take it easy."

"I'm sorry to contradict you, but as your nurse, I have to tell you that you're full of it." She glanced over at him. "Tell me that your ribs don't hurt."

"Hardly at all."

"You're not a very good liar, Flynt." She flashed him a grin. "There's another piece of information for you."

"That's funny," he said idly. "I've always thought I was a very good liar."

She glanced at him sharply, and saw him tense. "What do you mean?" she asked, her voice neutral.

"I have no idea." He looked over at her, his face stricken. "It just popped into my head that I'm a good liar."

"It doesn't mean anything," she finally said.

"Maybe, maybe not."

"Maybe you're an actor," she said desperately. "Actors have to be good liars. Or maybe you're a writer. They make things up all the time."

"Or maybe I'm a criminal."

Tina pulled into the parking lot of Tom's hotel and killed the engine. "You're awfully determined to think the worst of yourself. You need to stop being so stubborn. I thought you said that tiny bits of information don't mean a thing until you put them together. The same thing is true for this bit of information. Don't jump to conclusions."

He didn't move to get out of the car. Instead, he shifted in his seat so he was looking at Tina. "You're being pretty stubborn yourself, Tina. Why can't you face the facts? The chances are pretty good that I'm involved somehow in the Steele murders."

"That remains to be seen." She gripped her hands together and leaned toward him. "Maybe you ran out of the ball in order to catch the killer. Did you ever think of that?"

"Then why was I carrying a gun? And why did I have a fake driver's license and a fake address at my P.O. box?"

"I'm sure there was a good reason."

Tom laughed as he opened the door. "See? You're as stubborn as they come."

"Wait a minute," she said, scrambling out of the car. "Let me help you."

She hurried around to the passenger side of the car and wrapped her arm around Tom's waist. He leaned heavily against her as he pushed himself out of the car. Then he slowly straightened, but she knew he was still in pain from the stiff way he held himself.

"Maybe you should have stayed in the hospital for another day or two," she said, worried.

"I'll be fine. I'm just stiff because I was in bed for so long. Once I have a chance to move around a little, I'll be as good as new."

"I hope so." She looked at the impersonal facade of the hotel. She hated to think about him staying here, alone. What if he needed help during the night?

"I've got the key in my pocket," he said, reaching

for it. "Stone came by this morning and gave it to me."

"Let me get the door for you."

"I hate feeling helpless," he muttered.

"Somehow I could have guessed that about you." She fitted the key into the lock and pushed the door open. The apartment had the stale, untouched air of a house left empty for a while. Flicking on the lights, she stepped back and let him walk inside first.

"Not very exciting, is it?" he said after a moment.

She had to agree with him. One glance told her that there were very few personal belongings. The apartment didn't tell her a thing about its occupant. A stack of newspapers sat neatly on the coffee table. Nothing was out of place in the kitchen, and there were no pictures or mementos of any kind in the tiny living room.

"It's pretty basic," she said cautiously.

"Let's take a look around," he finally said. "Maybe we'll get some ideas."

They looked through the living area first, but aside from the stack of newspapers and a few paperback novels, there was nothing to give the room any hint of a personality.

"Well, at least we know you like to read," Tina said, holding the books. "And you have good taste in fiction." Tina smiled as she nodded at one book, a suspense thriller. "This woman started out writing romance novels. I've read every one of her books."

Tom stared at the books for a moment, then shook his head. "Nothing. I don't remember buying those books."

"Why don't we take a look in the kitchen?" she said.

The kitchen was even more dismal. The freezer held several microwave meals, and there was a package of cheese, a few eggs and some beer in the refrigerator.

"This is really depressing," Tina finally said. "What the heck did you eat?"

"I have no idea." Tom looked around, and the desolate expression on his face tugged at Tina's heart. "But this doesn't feel right," he said slowly. "This doesn't feel like home."

"It isn't your home," she pointed out. "The manager said you've only been here for a couple of weeks."

"That's long enough to make a place feel lived-in. Where's the clutter? Where's all my stuff?"

"Maybe you traveled light."

"So I could make a quick getaway?" He quirked an eyebrow at her.

"For heaven's sake," she snapped, "that's not what I meant."

"I know that. But maybe it's why there's nothing in this apartment."

"Or maybe it was because you were working long hours and were never home."

He smiled, and for the first time since they'd walked into the apartment, his eyes softened. "You're determined to look on the bright side, aren't you?"

"Someone has to do it," she retorted. "You're determined to see the worst."

"I have to be prepared for the worst," he said in a low voice. "Too many things point to my being involved in the Steele murders."

She shook her head. "You're not a criminal, Tom."

"You're the only one who doesn't think so," he said dryly, gesturing to the pile of unread newspapers that someone, probably the maid, had on the coffee table. "Even the papers have me pegged as a suspect."

The story on the front page was about Tom, the mystery patient at Vanderbilt Memorial Hospital. Tina picked it up. She hadn't seen that story. As she skimmed it, she saw with a sinking heart that the paper speculated that Tom was somehow connected to the murder of David and Lisa Steele.

"They don't know what they're talking about," she said, tossing the paper back onto the table.

He watched her for a moment, an unreadable expression in his eyes. Then he turned away. "I'm going to take a look in the bedroom."

Tina followed him to the door, then stood and watched him look around. She felt uncomfortable watching Tom search through his belongings in the bedroom. This was Tom's private space. He must feel as if everything about him was open to public scrutiny. He couldn't even recover from a serious car accident without everyone watching him, waiting to see what he remembered.

"Why are you standing there?" he said. "Come on in and take a look."

"I thought you might want a little privacy," she said.

"Why?" His voice was blunt. "You know as much about me as I do."

"That's exactly why. You must feel as if you're in a fishbowl. Everyone is watching you. This is your bedroom. I thought you might want some privacy."

He looked up from the dresser, where he was going

through the drawers. "That's very considerate of you, Tina." He shook his head. "It just proves what I've been telling myself for the last few days. You're too good and too kind to get involved with someone like me. You don't need this kind of trouble."

"What kind of trouble would that be?"

"The kind of trouble I might bring down on you," he said bluntly. "There might be warrants out for me in ten states."

"You might also be a very good man," she said. "That's the truth I'm betting on."

"The evidence doesn't point that way."

"The evidence can be taken more ways than one."

"Tell that to Detective Jones," he said, finally looking away.

"Detective Jones is doing his job," she said firmly. "You said so yourself." She watched him as he stepped away from the dresser. "Did you find anything in there?"

"Nothing but some clothes. There isn't anything that could give me a clue about my life before I came to Grand Springs. It's almost as if it were deliberate."

Her heart ached for him, standing in the middle of his cold, sterile apartment, nothing there that could give him a clue about his identity. "Come over to my house for dinner," she said impulsively. "Maybe a change of scenery will help."

As soon as the words were out of her mouth she regretted them. What was she thinking? She had never had a man over to her house. Her house was her refuge from the world, her safe haven.

But she couldn't leave him here by himself, in these depressing surroundings. So she took a deep breath. "We'll stop at the grocery and you can pick out something to eat. After five days of hospital food, you're probably ready for some real food."

"That does sound tempting." He looked over at her, and she could see the longing in his eyes. "But are you sure? I'm as close to a stranger as you can get."

Oddly enough, his reservations erased all of hers. "Of course I'm sure. And you're not a stranger. I've spent a lot of time with you in the last five days."

"All right then, I'd love to come to dinner." His mouth curved up in a smile. "Even a trip to the grocery store sounds exciting."

"You must be desperate," she said lightly. She wouldn't think about Tom in her house. Even the thought of it was too intimate and somehow disturbing. "Why don't we get going, then?"

"All right." He looked around the room one more time, then shook his head. "There's no reason to keep looking here. I don't feel any kind of connection to this apartment, or anything in it."

"Then let's get out of here."

They headed back to her car, and Tom bent to get into the passenger seat again. Already he moved more easily. Maybe he was right. Maybe all he needed was a little exercise to get his muscles moving again.

An hour later they pulled into the driveway of her home, and she turned off the engine and gathered herself. She had tried not to think about bringing Tom here, but she was nervous.

"I like your house," he said softly, staring out the window.

"Thank you." The small, two-story house was painted white with black shutters. A porch extended across the front of the house, complete with a swing.

She loved to sit there in the summer and enjoy her garden, but now the only flowers remaining were a few mums, the last bit of color bravely holding its own against the approaching winter.

"You've spent a lot of time on the house and the garden," he said.

"I love working in the garden."

"It shows." He turned to look at her. "You take care of your garden like you take care of your patients."

"Thank you." His eyes heated as he looked at her, and she hurried to get out of the car. "Come on in."

She stood in the doorway, watching him walk inside. He looked around for a moment, then turned to her. "It's great. Very peaceful and welcoming."

"Thank you," she said again, feeling foolish and very nervous. "You're welcome to sit down, or you can come into the kitchen while I get dinner ready."

"I'll help you get dinner ready."

"From the looks of that apartment, I'm not sure you can be trusted in the kitchen." It felt better to tease him. It lightened the atmosphere and took away some of the tension that seemed to stretch between them.

"Put me to work," he said. "I'll show you what I can do."

They talked easily while she prepared steaks and potatoes and Tom fixed a salad. She didn't say anything, but it was obvious he knew his way around a kitchen. Clearly, he had cooked before.

As they ate, he asked questions about Grand Springs, and she told him about the town. His questions were specific and detailed, and she thought that he seemed to be used to asking questions.

She mentioned that to him. "Do you think you might be a reporter of some sort?"

He thought about it for a moment, then shrugged. "I don't know. It doesn't sound familiar, but who knows?"

"Just a thought," she said lightly, and got up to get dessert. They had picked out an apple pie at the store, and she served them slices with vanilla ice cream.

"Do you want some coffee?" she asked.

"I'd love some."

She poured two cups, then said, "Why don't we have dessert in the living room?" She'd noticed that he'd shifted in his chair a couple of times. "The couch is probably more comfortable than these chairs."

"Thanks," he said, standing up slowly. "I guess I was stiffer than I realized."

"Your ribs will feel better every day. Don't forget, it's been less than a week since you were injured."

"I like having my own personal nurse," he teased.

"That means you have to do what I tell you," she shot back.

"Have you always been this bossy, or do I get special treatment?"

She watched him settle onto the couch, then set his coffee and pie down on the table next to him. "I'm not in the habit of feeding dinner to my patients."

"I didn't think so," he said quietly. "Thank you, Tina. I appreciate this, more than I can tell you."

"It's not a big deal." She spoke quickly. "I had to fix dinner anyway."

"It's a very big deal." His eyes warmed, and she thought he was going to say something, but then he looked away. When he looked back at her, there was only polite interest in his eyes. "Did you say you'd lived in this house all your life?"

The frustration that flooded in was a surprise to her. She should be grateful that he'd chosen safer conversational waters. So she swallowed once and nodded. "I grew up in this house. I lived here with my mother until she died eight months ago."

"I'm sorry," he said, sympathy in his eyes. "That wasn't very long ago."

"No, it wasn't. We were very close."

He touched her hand. "What about your father?"

She felt herself stiffen and forced herself to relax. "He died when I was twelve years old."

"I'm sorry," he said again. "Do you have any brothers or sisters?"

"No. I was an only child." She jumped up. "Do you want more coffee?"

He glanced at his cup in surprise. He hadn't taken a sip yet. "No, thanks. I'm fine."

"I'm going to freshen mine. I'll be right back."

Tina hurried into the kitchen and took a deep breath. She lifted the coffeepot, but her hands were shaking too much to pour the hot liquid. She set it back on the counter and closed her eyes.

What had she been thinking? She should never have brought him back here. They wouldn't sit and stare at each other all evening. They would talk. Of course the subject of her life would come up. It was only natural that he would ask about her parents.

She should have been prepared, but she wasn't. No one asked about her father anymore. No one even mentioned his name. It had been so long ago that most people had forgotten all about him. And what had happened.

But Tom would have no way of knowing that. He couldn't possibly know about her father.

She turned on the cold water and splashed it on her face. Having him ask about her father was the best reminder she could have had. She didn't get involved with men. She made it a point to stay away from men who had the hint of danger that Tom carried.

She especially didn't get involved with men who carried guns.

Standing up straight, she dried her face and picked up her coffee cup, then walked back into the living room. Tom watched her, concern on his face.

"I'm sorry. Did I say something to upset you?"

"It wasn't your fault. I guess I'm still grieving for my mother." It was the truth, but it wasn't what had upset her. She couldn't tell him about her father.

He set his coffee cup on the table and reached for her hands. "I can't even imagine how hard it must be for you. It sounds like it was just the two of you for a long time."

"Thank you. It has been hard."

"And you don't have any siblings to share it with."

"No." She looked at him. "What about you? Do you think you have any siblings?"

He shook his head. "I don't know. I hope so." He shrugged. "I don't like the thought of not having any connections in this world."

His words struck her, and she nodded slowly. "I think that's part of my grief for my mother," she said quietly. "Now I'm alone in the world. It's a little overwhelming."

"I know."

"I'm sorry," she said, grasping his hands more tightly, feeling stricken. "I shouldn't have said that. It was really insensitive of me."

"Don't worry about it. My situation is temporary, I hope."

"I hope so, too." She forced herself to put her own emotions out of her mind. "Do you want to talk about Grand Springs? See if something sounds familiar?"

He hesitated, then finally nodded. But she thought she saw disappointment in his eyes. "Were you at the ball when the Steeles were killed?"

She shook her head. "I was working at the hospital. Which was a good thing, because they needed all the hands available when the injured people started coming in."

"Did any of them talk to you?"

"Most of them did. They were terrified. What happened at the ball was both horrifying and frightening."

"What did they tell you?" He leaned forward.

"No one saw the actual murders. But they heard the gunshots and saw a man running with a duffel bag." She hesitated, then added, "And most of them saw you running after him."

"Did any of them know me?"

"Not that they told me. And I'm sure that Detective Jones has asked that same question. If any of them had known you, I'm sure he'd have let you know."

"You said there were a lot of patients that night. Did the killer shoot other people besides the Steeles?"

"No, he must have shot David and Lisa, grabbed

a duffel bag that David was carrying, and ran away. The other patients were hurt in the stampede that happened after the shooting. Most of the injuries were fairly minor, thank goodness.''

Tom brooded about what she had told him. Then he said, ''That's not much help.''

''I know.'' She looked at him with sympathy. ''But in a couple of days, when you're feeling better, you can look around Grand Springs yourself and see if anything looks familiar.''

''I'll do that.'' Tom leaned closer and searched her face. ''How can I ever thank you, Tina?''

It was hard to breathe. She stared at Tom, saw the heat in his whiskey-colored eyes, and felt herself tremble. ''No thanks are necessary.''

''This isn't standard procedure for all your patients,'' he said, and the light in his eyes changed. She recognized the change immediately, although she had very little experience with it. It was desire.

He stared at her as he bent closer, and she couldn't move, couldn't breathe. The next instant, he touched his lips to hers.

Chapter 6

Tina's first reaction was surprise. She hesitated as Tom's mouth brushed hers gently. Then, as his lips settled on hers, she instinctively moved closer, as unfamiliar sensations coursed through her.

Her heart began to pound and her skin felt far too sensitive. Tom touched her cheek with his hand, and she shivered. Ripples of pleasure started in her abdomen and flowed outward, engulfing her.

Then Tom groaned and wrapped his arms around her, pulling her closer. His chest felt hard and solid against hers, and her breasts tingled beneath the sweater she wore. He splayed his hand on her back, and she felt each of his fingers, every tiny change in pressure as he touched her.

A small voice in her head ordered her to stop, told her she was asking for trouble. But she ignored it. She couldn't pull herself away from the sensations crashing over her. She felt like she was drowning, and she welcomed the oblivion.

"Tina," he gasped, lifting his mouth from hers. She forced her eyes open to find his gaze on her face, his eyes filled with desire. "Tell me to stop."

The voice in her head urged the same thing, but the newly awakened passion thickening her blood was too powerful to deny. "I don't want to stop," she whispered. She reached out to touch him, her hand tentative, and he grabbed her hand and placed it on his chest. She could feel his heart thundering against her fingers.

"I've wanted to kiss you since the moment I woke up in the hospital and saw you looking down at me," he said, his voice thick. "And I know I have no right."

"You have whatever rights I give you," she said, her voice fierce.

He groaned again and crushed her mouth beneath his. This time his kiss wasn't gentle and tentative. He held her head with both hands and plundered her mouth, sweeping inside with his tongue when she gasped. Tina's heart pounded and her hands shook. Tom was drawing her into a vortex of passion, a strange and alien place that she'd never encountered before.

She was standing on the edge of a cliff, and she wanted to jump off the edge, she realized. She wanted to hand control over to Tom, to go wherever her passion took her. The knowledge was like an icy slap in the face. All her fears, all her caution came rushing back in one overwhelming wave. She jerked away from him, panting, staring at him with shock.

He opened his eyes to look at her, and the passion

faded from his eyes, replaced by concern. He reached for her hand. She flinched and tried to draw away, but he held onto her.

"What's wrong?" he whispered.

"I'm sorry," she said, swallowing hard. But she continued to meet his eyes. She refused to be a coward. "I guess you just took me by surprise."

Tom studied Tina and the expression in her eyes. There was much more than surprise in her face. Tina was afraid.

Of him.

The knowledge was like a blow to his chest.

"I'm sorry," he said, easing away from her, but continuing to hold her hand. "I should never have done that." He gave her what he was sure was a ragged smile. "I had no right to touch you. I'm glad you were smart enough to realize that."

Tina shook her head. "That's not it," she whispered. "It's not you, Tom."

"Then what is it?"

She looked away from him then. "I guess I'm just cautious about getting involved with men. I wasn't expecting you to kiss me."

There was more than caution in Tina's face. There was naked fear. It was more than a fear of him. It was almost as if she were afraid of the emotions she had felt. He wondered why, but knew he couldn't ask right now. She was already feeling too vulnerable. He saw the raw emotion in her eyes.

He couldn't push her over that edge. But he would find out the truth, sooner or later.

"It's okay," he murmured. "I guess I'm a little impulsive."

He watched her try to pull herself together. "Another piece of information to add to the puzzle," she said with a strained smile.

"You got it." He turned her hand in his and pressed a kiss into her palm. When he felt her tremble, his own desire came back in a rush. He wanted to kiss her again, and keep on kissing her.

Hell, he wanted to do a whole lot more than kiss her. And he knew he couldn't.

He had no right. He had nothing to offer her.

She swallowed once and pasted a smile on her face. He was sure it took every fiber of her will.

"Do you want some more coffee or pie?"

"No thanks," he said easily. "I should probably head back to my apartment. Don't you have to work tomorrow?"

"No, I'm off tomorrow, but I have a lot of errands to run." He saw the gratitude on her face. "And you're probably tired. It is your first day out of the hospital, after all."

"I am tired." He was exhausted, but he had a feeling he wouldn't be getting much sleep tonight. Tina was a puzzle, and he desperately wanted to put the pieces together. Almost as much as he wanted to put together the pieces of his own puzzle.

"Do you want me to take you back to your apartment now?"

"That probably would be best." He gave her a small smile. "I don't want to overstay my welcome."

"You couldn't do that." Her words were sincere, and he saw a flash of longing in them, quickly hidden. "You're welcome any time."

"Thank you, Tina. That means a lot to me."

She scrambled off the couch and reached for her

jacket. "It's going to be chilly outside. Do you want a sweatshirt or something?"

"I'll be fine."

"Your ribs are going to hurt more if you get cold and then tense up. Let me get you a sweatshirt."

Without waiting for him to answer, she ran up the stairs. Moments later she was back again with a faded gray sweatshirt with Colorado State blazoned on the front. It was plenty big for him and sudden jealousy speared him. Had it belonged to an old lover?

"This looks kind of big for you," he said, trying to make his voice light and teasing. He was probing to see if she would tell him who the sweatshirt belonged to, and he was ashamed of himself. He held his breath, waiting for her answer.

"I like my sweatshirts roomy," she said, not looking at him.

It was a non-answer, and he wished he had the right to ask her point-blank if the shirt had belonged to another man. But he didn't have that right. So he slipped the well-worn garment over his head, realizing that it carried her subtle, sweet fragrance.

"Thank you," he said, watching her. "It probably is getting a little chilly."

She gave him a strained smile. "Clearly you don't remember Colorado weather. It's downright cold at night in November. In fact, it's already snowed up in the mountains."

"I'll have to make sure I have some warm clothes," he said lightly. "Shall we go?"

The ride back to his hotel was strained. Although he tried, Tom couldn't suppress his desire for her. It pulsed between them in the darkened car, held in check only by his bewilderment at her strange reaction. He might not remember anything about his past life, but he was certain that fear wasn't a usual reaction to a kiss.

It was part of the mystery of Tina, and he wanted badly to solve it. But perhaps it was just as well, he told himself. He had no business kissing Tina, or doing anything else with her, until he regained his memory. He had no idea if he was even free to kiss her.

He didn't feel married, or attached in any way, but he couldn't trust his perceptions. He had no idea what they were based upon. So he stared out the window at the darkened town and tried to think about something else.

"Here we are," she said, a few minutes later, pulling into the parking lot. He could hear the strain in her voice. She was probably damn glad to be rid of him this evening. "Let me help you into the apartment."

"I can manage on my own."

He got the first real smile from her since he'd kissed her. "I know you think you can. But you did a lot today, considering that you were just released from the hospital. I want to make sure you're okay."

Without waiting for an answer, she jumped out of the car and came around to the passenger side. She helped him out of the car, and in spite of his efforts to control himself, his pulse jumped when she wrapped her arm around his waist.

She must have felt his reaction, because she stepped away from him and kept out of arm's reach as soon as he was upright. She walked next to him, but she held herself stiffly and was careful not to touch him as they headed for the door.

When he stepped inside, he turned to invite her in.

But before he could say anything, she shook her head. "I have to run, and I'm sure you want some time to yourself." She rummaged in her purse and took out a small notebook and a pen. She wrote something on a piece of paper, and handed it to him. "Here's my phone number. Call me if you need anything, even if it's in the middle of the night." She gave him what he was sure she thought was a casual smile. "I keep odd hours, and chances are I'll be awake."

"I'll do that." He took the paper without taking his eyes off her face. "Thanks again, Tina. Dinner was wonderful. I enjoyed spending time with you."

For a moment, the panicked fear was back in her face, then it was gone. "I enjoyed it, too. I'll talk to you tomorrow, all right?"

"Sounds good."

She hesitated, standing in the doorway for another long moment, then she nodded. "Sleep well, Tom."

"You, too," he said softly.

She turned around and walked to her car. She lifted her hand briefly in salute before she drove out of the parking lot. He watched until her taillights had disappeared into the distance, then he slowly closed the door.

"You screwed up big-time," he said to himself as he turned and looked at the barren apartment. "You'll be lucky if she comes within twenty feet of you again."

He desperately hoped it wasn't true. But the fear on her face was still vivid in his mind, and he eased himself down onto the couch, wondering about it.

Why had Tina been frightened by their kiss? She had claimed she didn't think he was a criminal. She had been adamant in defending him, in putting the best possible spin on what had happened. So why was she suddenly afraid of him?

She would have to be crazy *not* to be afraid of you, he told himself roughly. Why would she want to get involved with a man who had no memory, who was more than likely a criminal of some sort?

There was a big difference in being kind to someone and getting involved with them, he reminded himself. Even the most impulsive person would have to think twice about a relationship with a man who had no memory. And Tina was far from impulsive. In fact, he suspected she thought long and hard about any decisions she made.

"It's a good thing she was keeping her head," he muttered. "Because I sure wasn't keeping mine."

And it was a sign of his sorry state of mind that he was sitting in this empty apartment, talking to himself. It was time to go to bed.

But he lay in bed, awake, for a long time. The memory of Tina's mouth, how she had tasted, and how she had felt, her quick, involuntary surrender to him, tormented him far into the night. And the memory of her fear, and her trembling reaction when she'd realized what was happening, played over and over in his mind.

When he finally fell asleep, he was restless and edgy, awakened frequently by disturbing dreams. Tina's image flashed in and out of them, but when he tried to touch her, she danced out of his reach. By the time he woke in the morning, he was in a foul mood. And the stiffness that assaulted him when he tried to climb out of bed told him it was going to be a very long day.

* * *

By late morning he was certain he was about to go out of his mind. Dr. Wilson had told him not to even think about driving for another few days, so he hadn't left the apartment. He'd been stuck inside, looking for clues to his identity, and nothing had helped him. He'd been certain that if he stared at his belongings long and hard enough, they would give up their secrets.

But the pitifully few things in the apartment had been mute.

He was about to start over in his search when the doorbell rang. Easing himself off the couch, he told himself that it was probably Detective Jones, come to bring him more bad news. And in his present mood, he thought sourly, he was almost looking forward to it.

But when he opened the door, he found Tina standing on the small stoop. She looked nervous.

"Come in," he said, aware that his heart had begun to thunder in his chest. "What brings you over here?"

She stepped inside the door. "I realized that you weren't supposed to drive. I wondered if there was anything you needed from the store." She watched him carefully, reserve in her eyes.

"I hadn't thought about it, but I suppose I do." He gave her a grim smile. "As you pointed out, there isn't much here to eat."

"I was on my way to the grocery store," she said. "You're welcome to come along."

"I'd love to. I think I'll go crazy if I stay in this apartment for another minute."

The reserve faded, replaced by warmth. "I understand, I think. You assume that your belongings should help you figure out who you are, but it's just frustrating you. Right?''

"Absolutely. And the harder I try, the less I remember."

She thawed even more and laid a hand on his arm. "Dr. Mellon warned you about that, didn't she? I know she told you not to try and force it."

"I don't think I've ever been good at following orders," he said, then froze. "There, I did it again. I have no idea where that came from."

"Another small piece of the puzzle," she said lightly.

"And another suspicious one." His voice was grim. "Add that to the fact that I thought I was a good liar, and it's not a pretty picture that's emerging."

Tina shook her head. "There are a lot of people who aren't good at following orders, and most of them aren't criminals." She watched him for a moment, and he thought her expression softened. He wondered if she was even aware of it. "Get your coat," she finally said. "You can pick out some healthy food to eat."

Tina relaxed as Tom turned away to find a jacket. She'd told herself all day to stay away from him. After last night, spending time with Tom would be asking for trouble. But she couldn't stop thinking about him alone in that barren, lifeless apartment. And when she'd left to do her errands, she'd found herself turning into the parking lot without ever consciously making the decision to do so.

It didn't mean anything, she told herself firmly. She was just trying to be a good neighbor. The way his kiss had made her feel had nothing to do with it.

She'd already decided that she would forget about it and move on.

Except that she hadn't been able to forget about it. Tom had haunted her dreams the night before and shadowed her thoughts since she'd woken up. And she hadn't been able to suppress the excitement that built inside her as she'd walked up to his door.

"I'm ready," he said with a smile, and her heart lurched.

"Let's go, then," she said lightly. *Settle down,* she told herself. *Don't be a fool.* She knew she couldn't allow herself to get involved with Tom. He was everything she had warned herself against for far too long.

But he was also everything she had secretly dreamed of for even longer. And that frightened her even more than the kiss.

"On your day off, I thought you would do something more exciting than go to the grocery store," Tom said, as they pulled out of the parking lot.

She relaxed a little bit. Maybe he wasn't going to say anything about last night. "I have to eat," she said lightly. "And I want to stop by a bookstore later."

He turned to her, an arrested expression on his face. "Would you mind if I came along?"

"To the bookstore? Of course not." She glanced over at him, and the expression on his face made her chest tighten. "Did you remember something?"

Slowly, he shook his head. "No. But I have this strange feeling that I want to go to a bookstore."

"Do you want to go there right now?"

"I don't want to disrupt your schedule."

Tina laughed and slowed down to make a turn. "Trust me, I'll take any excuse to go to a bookstore."

"I do trust you," he said quietly. "Completely."

The smile faded from Tina's face. "You shouldn't do that," she answered. "You really know nothing about me."

"I think I know everything I need to know. You're kind, you're generous to a fault, and you're a warm, loving woman."

His words were small darts that embedded themselves in her heart. She shook her head. "Believe me, Tom, there's a lot more to me than that."

"Then fill me in. Tell me what I'm missing."

Tina saw the bookstore and pulled into the parking lot, infinitely grateful for the distraction. "It's a long, boring tale, and there are a lot more interesting stories in here," she said, trying to make her voice light and teasing. "Let's go find some of them."

She felt him watching her as she parked the car, but she didn't look at him. Instead, she jumped out of the car and came around to open his door. He got out of the car a lot more easily this morning.

They started heading for the store, and Tom said quietly, "I want to know everything about you, Tina. Both what's on the surface and what's underneath."

"I don't want to bore you with my life story," she said as she pulled open the door.

"Believe me, I won't be bored. That's the last word I would associate with you."

She knew he was watching her, but she didn't dare look at him. She shoved her hands into her pockets and looked around the large bookstore instead. "Here we are. What do you want to look for?"

Tom continued to stare at her for another moment,

then looked away. "I'm not sure," he said. "I have no idea, really. But when you said bookstore, it felt like a place I wanted to go."

Hoping she could maintain her composure, she finally looked at him. "You tell me what you want to do. Do you want me to stay with you? Do you want to roam around the store by yourself?"

But he wasn't looking at her. He was staring around the store, an arrested expression on his face. "Why don't you go ahead and get what you came for? I'll look around for a while by myself."

"Fine. I'll look for you when I'm finished."

Tom wandered off, but instead of looking at the romance and mystery sections of the store, as she had planned, she watched him move through the aisles. Every once in a while he stopped to pick up a book. He would look at it for a few moments, then replace it on the shelf.

Finally, he came to a stop in front of a tall bookcase. He reached out, picked up another book and stood reading it, apparently absorbed in the story, for a long time. Tina looked up to see what section it was, and her heart sank.

It was the true crime section.

Her hands shook as she fumbled with some books in the mystery section. She grabbed a few more selections from the romance shelves, then went to pay for her books. When she had finished, she looked for Tom. He was still in the true crime section of the store.

"Did you find what you wanted?" she asked as she walked up to him.

He looked up with a start. "I'm not sure. I got this

far and found this book, and I haven't been able to put it down."

"A high recommendation," she said lightly. "Are you going to buy it?"

He closed the book and tucked it under his arm. "I think so. But I'm still not sure why I wanted to come here."

"Maybe it's as simple as the fact that you like to read."

"Maybe so." He didn't look like he believed that. "Do you mind if I look around a little more?"

"Of course not." She smiled, although it was an effort. "I never complain about spending time in a bookstore."

They walked around for a while longer, then Tom stopped and shook his head. "I have no idea why I wanted to come here. But it seemed important at the time."

"You found a book," she said, nodding at the volume under his arm. "Maybe that's all it was."

"I have several books in my room."

"Maybe you've read them already."

"How would I know?" He gave her a grim smile. "I guess that's one of the positive things about amnesia. You can read your whole library again, and enjoy it just as much the second time around."

"I like a man who looks at the positive side of things," she said lightly, her fear for him receding. His choice of reading material didn't seem as important as the pain he was suffering. So what if he liked to read true crime books? There were a lot of other people who enjoyed them, too. And they weren't criminals, either.

He bought his book with one of the credit cards in

his wallet, and they walked out of the store. "Why do you think I went straight to the true crime section?" he asked.

"Because you like to read that type of book," she answered promptly. "Just like I go to the romance and mystery sections."

His mouth quirked up in a half smile. "I should have figured you'd say that. Of course you aren't going to tell me it's because I'm a criminal and want to read about my exploits."

"Don't be ridiculous." Her voice was firm. "You're clearly a reader and you simply wanted a book. Don't make more of it than that."

"I'll try not to."

They headed for the grocery store, talking about the town of Grand Springs. Tina was careful to avoid the topic of his choice of reading material, and was even more careful not to say anything about the night before. When they had finished shopping, she took him back to his apartment and helped him carry his groceries into the tiny kitchen.

He stood back and looked at the groceries lining the counter. "I'm never going to be able to eat all of this," he said. He turned to her. "Why don't you come over for dinner tonight and help me out?"

Tina told herself to say no. Tom was getting better. He was able to manage on his own. It was time to back away.

But she nodded and said, "I'd love to."

Chapter 7

Tina gripped the steering wheel as she drove toward Tom's apartment that night. What had she been thinking?

It was the same question she'd been asking herself all day. After last night, she needed to stay away from Tom. He tempted her far too much. And he was the last man she should get involved with.

If she got involved with anyone, it would be someone safe. Someone she had known for a long time, someone she knew everything about. Someone who would never surprise her.

Some nice, dull man who would bore her to tears within a month, a small voice inside her said.

Boring was good, she told herself firmly. Boring was safe. And Tom was anything but boring and safe.

Which was why she needed to stay away from him. She would never get involved with a man who reminded her even a little bit of her father.

Not that Tom was anything like her father. She didn't think Tom would hurt her, and he was certainly not an alcoholic. But Tom was dangerous in his own way. She suspected that she wouldn't be able to predict everything he would ever say or do. And she wouldn't be able to control him.

It hadn't been smart to accept his dinner invitation.

But he had seemed so alone that morning when she walked into his apartment. So lost in a strange town. She couldn't force herself to abandon him.

It would be easier to be at his apartment, she told herself. She would be less vulnerable there. There would be no memories to haunt her, no ghosts lingering in the air. She wouldn't be tempted to break down and tell him her life story. And she could leave whenever she felt like it.

By the time she pulled into his parking lot, she felt much better. Filled with confidence, she walked up to his door and knocked. But when he opened the door and smiled at her, her confidence vanished in a flash. Her breath whooshed out and her heart slammed against her chest. She swallowed once, hard, before she walked in.

He no longer looked like a hospital patient. In fact, he looked like the picture of health. His pallor was gone and there was a spring in his step. His eyes crinkled at the corners when he grinned at her, and a dimple flashed briefly in his right cheek. "Come in," he said. "I've been slaving over a hot stove for ages, and I'm looking for an excuse to put my feet up."

When she walked into the apartment, she smelled the heavenly scent of spaghetti sauce simmering on the stove. "It smells wonderful in here," she said.

His smile dimmed. "I wish I could say it was

Mother Flynt's secret recipe, but I'm afraid I just threw it together.''

''I'm sure it will taste fine.'' She stood and looked around. Even the apartment seemed to have lost some of its desolate air. ''Something is different in here.''

He came to stand beside her. ''I walked across the street to that discount store and bought a few cheap pictures. At least the walls don't look so bare now.''

''I like it,'' she said, turning to him. ''It feels more like a home.''

''I figured I might be here for a while.'' He searched her face, but didn't say anything more. ''Would you like a glass of wine, or a beer?''

''No thank you,'' she said. ''I don't drink.''

''I don't either right now,'' he said, turning back to the stove. ''There were some beers in the refrigerator, but I don't want to muddle my brain any more than it already is.''

''What can I do to help?'' she said, moving into the tiny kitchen. It brought her disturbingly close to Tom, but it would have been churlish not to offer.

''Why don't you slice the bread?'' he said, nodding toward the loaf of French bread he'd purchased earlier. ''Everything else is just about ready.''

Her arm bumped into him occasionally as she worked, and every time she pulled away with a jerk and muttered an apology. She felt her face flushing and heat swept up from her toes, but Tom didn't seem to notice. When she found herself wishing that Tom would move closer, she stopped slicing the bread and stepped abruptly out of the small kitchen.

''That should be enough bread,'' she said.

Tom nodded. ''Why don't you put it on the table?''

he said without looking at her. "I'll get everything else."

The width of the table separated them at dinner, and Tina relaxed a little. Again they talked about Grand Springs, and Tom encouraged her to talk about her life here. He said it would make it easier for him to visualize the town.

After dinner, they moved to the couch. Tina carefully sat at the far end, and watched as Tom sat down in the middle. She let out the breath she'd been holding. He was far enough away that it would be hard for them to touch accidentally.

"How long have you been a nurse?" he asked, leaning back against the cushions.

"For about four years now," she said, some of her tension disappearing. This was a safe conversational topic.

"And you like it?"

"I love it," she said simply. "It's a wonderful job."

"You're very lucky," Tom said quietly. "You're fortunate to love what you do."

"I know."

There was silence for a while, but it was a comfortable silence, and Tina felt herself relaxing even more. Then Tom said, "Do you want to talk about your mother?"

Tina was surprised by the question, but was even more surprised to find that she *did* want to talk about her. "Why do you think I would?"

He shrugged. "You take care of people every day, but I wondered if there was anyone to take care of you. You live alone, you don't have any siblings, so you probably haven't had anyone to talk to about your mother.''

''That's very perceptive of you.''

He took her hand. ''You've done a lot for me, Tina. It makes me wonder who takes care of you.''

Tears thickened in the back of her eyes. ''You know, if someone had asked me this morning if I wanted to talk about my mother, I would have told them no. But I want to tell you about her.''

He turned to face her on the couch, holding onto her hand. ''I want to listen.''

She spoke slowly at first, telling him how close she had been to her mother. ''It was just the two of us,'' she said. ''We've always been closer than most mothers and daughters. I grew up relying on her.''

''Especially after your father died, I imagine.''

''It was just the two of us even before he died.'' She clamped her lips together, appalled that that had slipped out. She wouldn't discuss her father with Tom.

''She got sick about three years ago. She had breast cancer, and it was very aggressive. She found it pretty early, but it had already spread.'' She stopped speaking, trying to compose herself. ''I began working the evening shift about a year and a half ago. That way I could be with her during the day, and we had a nurse in to stay with her while I worked. She mostly slept during the afternoon and evening, anyway.''

''I'm sorry,'' he said, moving closer and wrapping an arm around her. ''I wish I had known you then.''

She found herself wishing that he had, too. The weight of his arm on her shoulders was solid and comforting. It felt wonderful to tell him about her mother. ''It was hard. She was always cheerful, and that made it even worse. Right before she died, I took a leave of absence from work. I'll always be grateful to the hospital for being so understanding.''

''And you've had to get over her death on your own.''

''I love my job,'' she said. ''That helped.''

She didn't tell him that she would have done anything for her mother. Her mother had protected her from her father when she was younger. It had forged an unbreakable bond between them.

''But there was no one to hold you,'' he murmured, and he reached out and pulled her into the circle of his arms. ''No one to comfort you. I'm sorry about that.''

She leaned into him, grateful for his warmth, for the solid feel of his chest against hers. He held her gently and smoothed his hand down her hair. She hadn't known how comforting a man's arms could be.

Tom's hand moved down her back, soothing and reassuring. But Tina felt his fingers trembling, then realized that Tom's muscles were tense against hers. She leaned back to ask him why, but the words died in her throat. Even though she had very little experience with men, she had no trouble reading the expression in his eyes.

It was undiluted desire, hot and potent. When he met her gaze, his eyes darkened to a deep brown.

''Tina,'' he whispered.

Instead of pulling away, she stared at him. Her heart pounded in her chest and thundered in her ears. She was certain he could hear it, certain that he knew how he was affecting her.

She ignored the little frisson of fear that trembled

through her. She trusted Tom. He wouldn't hurt her. She knew that much, at least.

"Aren't you going to move away?" he asked.

Slowly, she shook her head. "No," she said, in a voice she barely recognized as her own. She might be making a huge mistake, but she didn't want to move away from Tom. She wanted to feel his hands on her, to feel his mouth on her lips again.

His eyes blazed, then he framed her face with his hands. "I want to kiss you, Tina. May I?"

She nodded without taking her eyes off his. His pupils dilated, and then he bent his head to touch his lips to hers. He kissed her gently, softly, brushing his mouth against hers and being careful not to kiss her too deeply.

A curl of desire unfurled inside her. She shifted her head and tried to kiss him back, but he nibbled at her lower lip until she moved restlessly against him.

She thought she felt him smile against her mouth, but when she lifted her head, he brushed his lips against her cheek. "Can I kiss you again, Tina?"

"Yes, please," she said, her voice breathless.

This time, his mouth settled against hers and she felt herself straining toward him. When he touched his tongue to her lips, she opened her mouth to him, hungry for his taste.

Every bit of her felt like it was on fire. When he eased her down onto the couch, she lifted her arms and pulled him close. She felt him shudder, and then he deepened his kiss. Tina felt like she was drowning in sensation. She wrapped her arms around him and held on, suddenly needing to feel his body against hers.

Her breasts throbbed and ached, and she jumped

when Tom brushed his hand over her chest. But when he touched the side of her breast gently, letting his fingers travel in a lazy circle, she wanted to shift her body so he was touching more than just the side of her breast. She longed to feel his hands on her, touching her, caressing her.

"Please," she moaned.

Tom froze. "Do you want me to stop?"

"No," she whispered. "I don't want you to stop. I want you to...to touch me."

His body tensed and she realized he was trying to control his reaction to her. The knowledge made her throb and ache. Slowly he touched her breast, first just one finger, gently brushing over her nipple. When she trembled and curled her hands into his shirt, he took her whole breast in his hand.

She cried out at the unfamiliar sensations. Her head was spinning and her body ached and throbbed. She arched into him, desperate for more.

She heard his ragged breathing, felt his hand tremble. Then he slowly unbuttoned her blouse, and she felt the cool air on her overheated skin. In another second he'd unhooked the clasp on her bra, and she felt the skimpy material fall away from her body.

Her first reaction was to lift her hands to cover herself. Tom took her hands gently in his and pressed a kiss into each palm. Then he looked down at her. "Do you want me to stop?"

She opened her eyes and looked at him. Although passion blazed from his eyes, she knew that with one word from her, he would sit up and move away from her. The knowledge made her drop her hands to her sides. "No," she said, watching him, "I don't want you to stop."

The expression in his eyes shifted and changed, and she saw tenderness where there had been only passion before. Then he bent and kissed her beneath her breast. Her skin jumped and twitched, and he smoothed his hand over her ribs.

"I want to taste you, Tina," he murmured. Slowly he lifted his head, watching her as he took a nipple in his fingers. The pleasure was so intense that she gasped. "I want to taste every bit of you. But I want to start right here."

He bent and took her nipple into his mouth, and every ounce of common sense she possessed dissolved in the pleasure that washed over her. Sensation after sensation crashed through her, each wave more intense than the last. She tried to pull him closer, needed to feel him against the throbbing between her legs. When he lifted his head, she heard herself moaning his name.

"Tina," he gasped, and she saw the wild need that raged in his eyes, felt it in the trembling of his hands. Suddenly, she realized that his control was hanging by a thread.

She should have been frightened. Her rational self surfaced, told her to get up, push him away. But instead she tightened her arms around him.

She was drowning in pleasure, drugged with it. She hadn't known about this. In all the years that she'd avoided getting involved with men, she'd never known she could feel like this.

Tom must have seen the surrender in her eyes. He groaned her name and kissed her again. But the desperation was banked this time. Instead, he kissed her with a gentleness and a tenderness that moved her.

Then he sat up and lifted her up next to him. He pulled her blouse together and turned her to face him.

"I'm sorry," he murmured, cupping her face with his hands, and searched her eyes. "I got a little carried away. Once I kissed you, I didn't want to stop."

"I didn't want you to stop, either," she answered. She could give him honesty, at least.

"I know." His mouth curled into an intimate smile and he bent to kiss her again. "Believe me, Tina, I know. Stopping just then might have been the hardest thing I've ever done."

"Then why did you stop?"

"Because I have no right to touch you, let alone make love to you. I know nothing about myself, and neither do you. Regardless of what you think, the Grand Springs police have good reason to think I'm involved in a crime."

"I don't think you're a criminal," she said quietly. "I know better than that. But I guess I'm glad you stopped. I'm not ready to make that decision."

"I know you weren't ready. This has happened too quickly. We were thrown together in intense circumstances. And regardless of who you think I am, there's still a cloud hanging over me. Until it's resolved, I have nothing to offer you."

"I think you have plenty to offer, Tom. What just happened here is proof of that. Where you came from or who you are doesn't matter as much as what's inside of you. Only a man who is essentially good would have stopped tonight."

"You're making me sound like a saint, Tina. I'm damn sure I'm no saint. But I wouldn't take advantage of you, either."

The intense arousal that had gripped her was receding, and her common sense reasserted itself. "Thank you," she said quietly. "I guess it's a good thing one of us was thinking."

He looked down at her, and she could see the regret in his eyes. "Maybe you'd better go home before I change my mind," he said roughly.

A spark flared to life inside her, but she stood up. "You're right. I don't know what I was thinking." She gave a shaky laugh. "That's the problem. Thinking had nothing to do with what happened here tonight. I never planned on getting involved with anyone."

Curiosity sharpened in his eyes, and she thought he would ask her to explain. But instead, he stood up beside her and said, "Then I guess we both did the smart thing."

She didn't understand the regret, sharp and bitter, that she tasted in her mouth. She was making the right decision. "We did."

After promising that she would check on him again soon, she left and got into her car. The night was crisp and clear, with a sliver of moon shimmering in the cold air. She tried not to think about Tom as she drove home, but she couldn't stop herself. She was relieved, she thought, that he had stopped her from making a huge mistake.

But beneath the relief, the regret lingered. She couldn't help thinking that she had reached a vital turning point in her life, and she had turned the wrong way.

She was still thinking about Tom and not paying attention to her routine much later that evening as she prepared for bed. Even after she turned out the lights, she lay restless, the faint moonlight streaming through her window. Instead of falling asleep right away, she stared up at the ceiling for a long time, reliving what had happened earlier and her reaction to it.

The first time she heard the noise, it didn't register. Then she heard it again. It sounded like someone had stepped on the squeaky board on her front porch.

Was someone at her door? She sat up in bed and waited for the doorbell to ring. But the house stood silent and still. She strained to listen, but heard only the pounding of her heart in the blood rushing through her veins.

Then she heard another sound. This time it sounded like it came from the back of the house. Could she have a prowler?

Fear made her palms sweaty as she grabbed a robe and slipped out of bed. Had she remembered to lock her doors? Or had she been too distracted by what had happened with Tom that evening? She walked slowly down the cold stairs in her bare feet, stopping frequently to listen. She didn't hear anything but the pounding of her own heart. She watched the windows, looking for a shadow and afraid that she might actually see one.

By the time she reached the main floor, sweat dripped down her back and her skin felt clammy with fear. She checked the lock on the door, then forced herself to go to the front window and lift the curtain. There was no one at the front of the house. The street was empty, and so was her yard. Bushes and dead flowers threw odd shadows on the grass, but she saw nothing that looked like an intruder.

She watched for a long time, letting her heart slow down. Finally she let the curtain fall and walked into the kitchen. She stood by the kitchen window and braced herself to lift that curtain.

There was no one in the backyard, either. All the houses around her stood dark and still. No dogs barked, and no car engines started abruptly.

She let the curtain fall back into place and stood in the cold kitchen for a moment. Then she flipped on the lights and turned on the stove. She'd make herself some tea before she went back up to bed.

"It must have been your imagination," she told herself firmly out loud. "Or else the neighbor's cat was on your porch again."

By the time she finished her tea, she had convinced herself that she hadn't heard a thing. But she checked all the doors and windows again before she went back up to bed. And she slept lightly, waking at the slightest sound.

Tom paced in the small apartment, checking his watch again for the fourth time that hour. Tina had phoned and told him she would stop by on her way home from work that night. It was getting late, and he was worried.

He'd spent most of the day in the apartment and was ready to climb the walls. He needed to talk to Dr. Wilson. If he couldn't get a car and begin to drive around the city, he was afraid he would lose his mind. The small apartment was beginning to feel claustrophobic, and he chafed at the restrictions the doctor had placed on him.

For a while he'd even considered getting a car, regardless of what the doctor said. But he knew Tina would worry, so he told himself to be patient.

And speaking of Tina, where the hell was she? He

ran his hands through his hair and looked out the window one more time. He told himself that he was just worried because she was late, but it was more than that.

He missed her.

He hadn't seen her for the past twenty-four hours, and every minute of that time had felt like a year.

The intensity of his feelings shook him, but he told himself it was perfectly natural. He was in a strange town, he had no idea who he was, and Tina was his link to reality. Of course he missed her.

But there was far more to it than that, a small voice said. He missed Tina because of who she was, not because of what she represented. He missed her smile, her teasing, her warmth. He missed having her around.

A car pulled into the parking spot in front of his room and stopped, and he rushed to the door. She was only halfway to the door when he opened it.

"Hi!" She grinned at him, and he felt the tension evaporating.

"Hi, yourself. I was getting worried."

She laughed at him as she stepped inside and closed the door. "That's because you don't have anything better to do."

It was far more than that. He would worry about Tina whenever she wasn't around, he realized with a flash of insight.

But he wouldn't tell her that. "Do you have another mystery patient you're taking care of?" he teased.

"One of those is quite enough." She stood and looked at him, and her smile faded. "You really do look worried. Are you all right?"

"I'm fine, now that you're here." Oops, he didn't want to scare her off. "I mean, I was picturing the worst possible scenarios. Car accidents figured prominently in my thoughts."

She smiled again. "Nurses can't always leave the minute their shift is up. I'm sorry. I would have called if I had known you were going to worry."

"I'll know better next time." But he would still worry.

She sat down on the couch, and he was careful to sit far enough away from her that he couldn't easily reach out for her. He was still shaken by what had happened the night before. He hadn't imagined that he could react that strongly to a woman. The intensity of his feelings had unnerved him. And to be fair to Tina, he had vowed that it wouldn't happen again.

But seeing her now, sitting in the pool of light from the lamp, was making it hard to remember his vow.

Chapter 8

Her dark red hair gleamed in the light and her eyes were weary. He wanted to gather her close and wrap his arms around her. He wanted to soothe away her worries.

But he would settle for conversation. It was all he would allow himself. "You look tired. Was it a tough day at work?"

She shook her head. "Not particularly. At least no more so than usual. But I was up for a long time last night."

His heart leaped, but he struggled to control himself. "How come?"

She flashed him a shy smile, then looked away. "I think you know part of the reason. But that wasn't all." Her smile faded, and she looked at him again. "I thought I heard a prowler around my house last night."

"What?" He leaned toward her, fear clutching at

him. He couldn't identify its source, but a sudden, suffocating cloud of anxiety surrounded him. "What do you mean?"

"I had been in bed for a little while, but I wasn't asleep yet. I thought I heard someone on my front porch. One of the boards squeaks," she explained. "Then I thought I heard someone at the back door."

"What did the police say?"

She looked away from him. "I didn't call the police."

He slid closer and grabbed her wrist. "How come?"

"Because I thought I was hearing things. I went downstairs and looked around. I didn't see or hear a thing."

"What if there had been someone standing in your kitchen when you went down those stairs?" he asked, his voice rough. He was sick with fear. "What would you have done then?"

"Grand Springs is usually a very safe town," she answered, trying to draw her hand away from him. "The Steeles' murder was unusual. Things like that don't happen here."

"Things like that can happen anywhere." He didn't let her hand go. Instead, he twined their fingers together and brought her hand to his mouth without thinking.

"There was no one near my house, Tom," she said gently. "I looked."

"You should have called the police."

She watched him for a moment, then moved closer to him. "You're awfully upset about such a small thing."

He let her hand go and stood up to pace around the

room. "It doesn't feel like a small thing to me," he said. "Something about it really bothers me."

She cocked her head and watched him. "Does it have something to do with your memory?" she asked slowly. "Something to do with why you're here?"

"Maybe. I don't know." He pressed his hands against his head, hoping to force the memories to come. There was nothing but a deep, dark void. "I can't remember. But I don't like it."

"I made sure all the doors and windows were locked," she said, watching him. "And I listened and watched for a long time."

"Do you have a security system?" he demanded.

"No, of course not. I've never needed one before."

"I want you to get one." He was stunned at the intensity of his response, shocked and uneasy. He had no idea why the thought of a prowler at Tina's bothered him so much.

"I think you're overreacting, Tom," she said gently. "But if it happens again, I promise you that I'll consider a security system."

He sat back down beside her on the couch. "Why do I think you're only trying to appease me?"

"Because you're blowing this all out of proportion. Maybe there was someone on my front porch. But chances are it was a neighbor, hoping to find me awake, and who, when he or she didn't see any lights, left without knocking."

"No neighbor would look for you at that hour of the night," he said.

"My neighbors all know that I'm usually awake late."

She reached out and took his hand. Tom was surprised. He had noticed how careful she was not to touch him. "I appreciate the fact that you're concerned. But I really don't think there's anything to worry about. Okay?"

He nodded slowly, trying to suppress the fear that wanted to engulf him. There was some reason he was so alarmed. He just had to figure out what it was. "All right."

"I don't have to work tomorrow," she said, and he knew she was deliberately changing the subject. "Would you like the grand tour of Grand Springs? We can drive through town and maybe even get out and walk around. I'd be happy to take you to the hotel where the ball was held and the site of your car accident. Maybe seeing something familiar will shake some memories loose."

"I'm not sure about that. I've spent three days here in this hotel room and I haven't remembered a damn thing."

"It's worth a try," she said. "How about if I pick you up around eleven tomorrow morning?"

"That would be great," he said. He knew he had been negative. Then he added, "I'm sorry, but I'm worried about you going home alone."

"I'll be fine." She stood up. "I'll call you when I get home."

"I'll be waiting." He wanted to scoop her into his arms and hold on tight, but he stepped away and shoved his hands into his pockets. He had told her last night that he didn't have a right to touch her, and nothing had changed. But it didn't help to see the disappointment flicker in her eyes when he moved away.

"I'll see you in the morning, Tina," he said, opening the door. He didn't want her to leave, but if she stayed any longer, his good intentions would fly out the window. "And don't forget to call when you get home."

"I won't." She hesitated on the porch. "Good night, Tom," she finally said. He thought she wanted to say more, but she turned away and hurried to her car. The night air was cold, and he watched her breath form a cloud as she unlocked her car door. He wanted to walk out and kiss her goodbye, but instead he gripped the doorknob and waited for her to get into the car. Only then did he let go of the knob. He raised his hand in farewell and watched her drive away.

He couldn't sit down. He paced the room, calculating how long it would take for her to drive home, then get in the house and lock up. He was just about to call her himself when the phone rang.

"I'm home," she said.

"Thank God. Have you checked the house?"

"I'm going through it as we speak. That way, if there's an intruder, you'll hear me scream." He heard the teasing laughter in her voice.

Fear gripped him again, and he didn't answer. After a moment, she said, "I'm sorry, Tom. I shouldn't have said that." All the laughter was gone from her voice. "Please, forgive me. I'm not making fun of you. It's just that I'm not worried."

"I know," he muttered. "And I'm not sure why I am."

"I'll be careful." He heard a muffled noise, and then she was back. "I checked all the windows and they're all locked. So are all the doors."

"If you hear something tonight, will you promise me you'll call the police?"

"If it will make you feel better, I will," she said.

"Good." He took a deep, shuddering breath. "Even if you think it's a neighbor, or a cat."

"Even if I think it's harmless," she repeated. "I'll call the police."

"Good night, Tina. I'll see you in the morning."

"Good night." He heard the soft click of the phone disconnecting, but stood holding it in his hand for a while before he replaced it. He'd be damned if he'd be trapped in this hotel for another day. He was going to get a car tomorrow. He needed to be able to get to Tina's quickly if she needed him.

Tina was sure there was nothing wrong, he reminded himself. And he couldn't remember why he was sure there was. He sank down on the couch, trying to dredge up a reason, but all he could find was a deep-seated terror that wouldn't let go of him.

He was pacing the house when Tina arrived the next morning, a half hour before he expected her. He opened the door and ushered her inside.

"What happened last night? Did you hear anything?"

"Nothing. And this time I was listening for it."

"Thank goodness."

"Are you ready to go, or do you want to wait for a while? I'm early, I know. I figured you'd be worried about last night, so I thought I'd better get here ahead of time and let you know everything was okay."

"Thank you," he said, moved by her thoughtfulness. "I was worried. And I'm ready to go." He gave her a small smile. "It's not like I have lots of other things to do."

"Why don't we get started, then? Where would you like to go first?"

He thought for a moment, then said, "How about the place the ball was held?"

"The Grand Springs Empress Hotel," she said. "Let's go."

As they drove, he peppered her with questions about the hotel. Finally she held up her hand. "You can see it for yourself in a few minutes. It's a new hotel, less than three years old. We'll park and walk through the ballroom, although it's not going to look the way it did for the ball."

Tom stared out the window as they pulled into the grounds of the luxury hotel. The landscaping was carefully tended and the building gleamed in the morning sunlight.

A valet took the keys to Tina's car, and Tom frowned. "How much do you know about what happened here that night?"

"Only what other people have told me."

"Did I have the valet park my car?"

"I don't think so. Apparently you parked it yourself, close to the door. The witnesses said they heard the gunshots, saw one man running out the door and you followed almost immediately. They heard your car start just moments later."

"So I was watching him."

"Or waiting for him. Nobody knows exactly what happened. The detectives can probably tell you more."

"Okay, let's take a look."

They walked through the sumptuously decorated lobby, and Tina walked over to the concierge and asked a question. The woman pointed down a hall, and he saw Tina nod her thanks.

"The ballroom is right down this hallway," she said as she rejoined him.

"Let's take a look."

Tom tried to keep his mind blank, tried not to push himself to remember. It didn't matter. Nothing looked familiar. It merely looked like a large, impersonal luxury hotel, with the requisite chandeliers and elegant furniture and polished wood.

"Here's the ballroom," Tina said, as she opened the door.

They stepped inside. The room was a wide expanse of wood floor and mirrored walls. He walked to the center of the room and closed his eyes. There would have been people in fancy clothes, and an orchestra, and the murmurs of voices. There would have been the subtle blend of many perfumes and the rustle of silk and satin.

He opened his eyes and looked around, but all he saw were the blank walls and the empty space. There was no glimmer of recognition, no burst of memory.

Slowly he shook his head. "Nothing," he said to Tina, who was standing beside him.

He saw the disappointment on her face. "Do you want me to see if I can find pictures of that night? I'm sure there was a photographer here."

"Okay." But he wasn't sure it would help. This place had no resonance for him. It didn't tug at him. If he were going to regain his memory, it wouldn't happen here.

"Where would you like to go now?" she asked, taking his hand. She touched him almost hesitantly, as if she weren't sure of his response. Twining his fingers with hers, he brushed his mouth over their joined hands.

"Do you have any suggestions?"

"How do you feel about tracing the route you took that night after you left the hotel?"

"Do you know what it is?"

"The police are fairly sure where you went." She gave him a quick smile. "There aren't all that many places to go in Grand Springs."

"That sounds like a good idea."

They got back into her car and drove silently out of the grounds of the hotel. "You probably drove down the main street of town," she said as she maneuvered through traffic. "You were found on the outskirts of town, on this same street. So it would be logical to assume this is the way you went."

He nodded, looking out the window. It was as if he'd never been in this town before. And according to the police, he'd been here at least two weeks before the accident.

In only a few minutes, the houses had become scarce and the landscape had turned lonely and uninhabited. Tina pulled off the road and parked the car.

"Here we are," she said. "This is where they found your car."

He was reluctant to get out, but he embraced his hesitation. It must mean something. Slowly, he stepped out of the car. The wind was biting, and he zipped up his jacket as he stood and looked around.

There were faint skid marks on the pavement, which he studied. Tina came to stand next to him. "I called Stone Richardson to ask him exactly where your car was found," she said. "He told me that they thought the skid marks might have come from two different cars."

"You mean there was another car involved in the accident?"

"Possibly. But yours was the only car here."

He studied the faint black marks on the road, but they didn't tell him anything. Finally, fighting the uneasiness that gripped him, he said, "Where was my car?"

"Over here." Tina led the way through the tall weeds that grew at the side of the road. About ten feet from the pavement, there was an area where the weeds were crushed and trampled. There was a dark stain in the center, and he couldn't help staring at it.

"What's that?" he finally said.

"Probably fluids from the car," she said, squatting to look more closely. She turned to look up at him, and he saw the understanding on her face. "It's not blood, if that's what you think."

"That wouldn't bother me." He was surprised by the statement, but realized it was true. "I was wondering if it could help explain how the accident happened."

"It might." Tina stood up and brushed off her hands. "You should talk to Detective Richardson."

"I'll do that." Something stirred in his mind, a flicker of recognition. But it disappeared, and he couldn't force it to return. All that was in his mind was an edgy tension. "Let's go, Tina," he said abruptly. "I don't remember anything."

As they drove away from the accident scene, he turned in his seat to watch it disappear from sight. "How did they find me so quickly?"

"You were lucky," she said. "The police department had everyone available out looking for the two men who ran away from the ball. The officer who found you noticed that the weeds were crushed by the side of the road. He thought that the killer might have driven off the road to hide, so he went looking. That's when he found you.''

"What were the damages to my car?'' he asked abruptly.

"I don't know. You'll have to talk to the detectives to find that out.''

"I will.'' He wasn't sure why it was important, but he wanted to know. "Where are we going now?''

"I thought we might park the car and walk around town a bit. That is, if you're up to it.''

"I'd like to do that. I think I'm going stir crazy after being confined to my hotel the last few days.''

They drove into downtown Grand Springs once again, and Tina parked her car. Then they started walking.

His ribs ached a little, but the crisp air tasted wonderful. "Thank you for suggesting this, Tina. I'm not sure it helped with my memory, but it's good to be moving around.''

"I thought you would enjoy it. You strike me as the kind of person who is active,'' she said idly.

"Why do you say that?''

She didn't look at him, and he saw a faint flush on her cheeks. "You're pretty fit. Your muscles are toned, you're not overweight. It's one reason why you're recovering so rapidly.''

"You're very observant.''

Her color deepened. "It's part of my job. We need to know a patient's level of activity, so we know how to help rehabilitate them after an accident.''

"And here I was hoping it was personal,'' he teased.

When she mumbled a reply, Tom realized that she wasn't really comfortable flirting with him. He wondered why. Tina was a beautiful woman and he was sure men had pursued her. But she had built fences around herself, and he was only just beginning to realize how high they were.

"Hey, you need to kick my butt if I get out of line," he said.

She flashed him a smile. "Don't worry. I won't hesitate."

They walked slowly through town, and as they waited to cross the light, someone walked up behind them. Tina looked over her shoulder, then turned around.

"Julie! How are you doing?"

"Pretty well," a soft voice said.

Tom turned around, and Tina grabbed his hand. "Julie, this is Tom Flynt. Tom, this is Julie Harrison. She's a teacher here in Grand Springs."

"Nice to meet you, Mr. Flynt."

The other woman, hugely pregnant, gave him a sweet smile, and Tina asked, "How are you feeling, Julie?"

She smiled and touched her abdomen. "Pretty well, actually. I can't believe the baby will be here in a month."

"Is there anything I can do? Anything you need?"

Julie hugged Tina. "It's wonderful of you to ask, but I think I'll be fine. You can be sure I'll call you if I need help."

"Make sure you do." Tina watched as her friend walked away, then turned back to Tom. "I worry about Julie being alone. She got divorced just recently. Her marriage fell apart when her husband cheated on her while she was pregnant.''

''What kind of a worm would do something like that?'' he frowned.

''The kind of worm Julie was married to.'' Tina scowled. ''She's better off without him.''

''It must be tough, though, to be pregnant and alone.''

''I'm sure it is. But she never complains.''

They continued to walk down the street, and Tom realized that the kindness and generosity Tina had shown him were an essential part of her. It just reinforced his determination not to do anything that would hurt Tina. She was too special. She didn't deserve the kind of grief she could be courting by getting involved with him.

''What else would you like to do?'' she asked.

''Are we far from the Grand Springs Police Department?'' he asked abruptly.

''A couple of blocks. Why?''

''I'd like to go talk to Detective Richardson again. Maybe something he says will trigger a memory.'' He *had* to find out who he was. For Tina's sake. Because he wasn't at all sure he was going to be able to stay away from her.

Chapter 9

Tina watched as Tom leaned across the desk in the police station. "Have you found out anything else, Detective Richardson?" he asked, his voice urgent.

The detective shook his head. "Nothing. I haven't been able to trace the driver's license, and the credit card company says you've been paying your bills on time."

"Where does the money come from?"

"They get a money order every month. They come from different banks, mostly in the Midwest. Completely untraceable."

"What about my fingerprints?"

"We haven't identified them yet."

Tom slumped back in his seat. "So you still have no idea who I am."

"That about sums it up." The detective's eyes filled with sympathy. "Listen, Flynt. I learned from my last case with an amnesiac that the more you push it, the longer it takes to remember. Just let it go. Don't worry about it.''

Tom scowled. "That's easy for you to say. You don't have possible criminal charges hanging over your head."

"True enough. But what else can you do?"

"I'll keep working on it."

"Don't work too hard." The detective looked concerned. "I'm serious, Flynt. You're just going to make yourself nuts."

"What would you do in my position, Detective?" Tom shot back.

Stone gave a short, sharp laugh. "Exactly what you're doing. But that doesn't mean it's the smart thing to do."

"It's what I'm going to do, though."

The detective nodded. "Good luck, then. If you think of anything that will help us find more information about you, let me know."

"And don't leave town," Tom added. "Right?"

"Right." Stone studied him for a moment. "You know the drill, apparently."

"I guess I do."

As they headed out into the cold air again, Tina grabbed his arm. "I know what you're thinking, and you're wrong." Her voice was fierce.

"What am I thinking?"

"You think that all that business about the money orders and your credit card payments being untraceable must mean that you're a criminal." She shook his arm. "You're figuring you might just as well save everyone a lot of trouble and turn yourself in right now." She turned to look in his face. "I'm right, aren't I?"

He scowled. "What am I supposed to think? All the evidence is pointing that way."

"You can take a look inside yourself." She shook his arm again, infuriated. "Do you think you're a criminal?"

"I don't know what I think, Tina. I have no idea."

She sighed, her anger gone. "I'm sorry, Tom. I lost my temper. But I can't bear to watch you beating yourself up."

Tom smiled, but the humor didn't linger in his eyes. His smile faded quickly. "It's good to know that someone believes in me," he said, his voice wistful. "Thank you, Tina, for that."

"You're welcome," she said, aware that she was holding his arm far too tightly and standing way too close to him. But when she tried to move away, he drew her closer.

"You know why I'm so determined to find out who I am, don't you?" he asked in a low voice.

"Of course. Everyone needs to know that."

"There's more to it than that. It wouldn't be so urgent if you weren't involved."

"What do you mean?" Her heart began to pound.

When he looked at her, she saw the desire in his eyes. "I'm attracted to you, Tina. Hell, I'm a lot more than attracted. But I don't have any right to get involved with you right now. I have nothing to offer you. I don't even know if Tom Flynt is my real name."

"I know a lot about you, Tom. I know you're a kind man, and a good one."

"Tina, I don't even know if I have a future," he said roughly. "What if I *was* involved in the Steeles' murders?"

Play

The

Lucky Hearts Game

and get...

FREE BOOKS & a **FREE** GIFT...
YOURS to KEEP!

Yes! I have scratched off the silver card.
Please send me my **2 FREE BOOKS**
and **FREE MYSTERY GIFT**. I understand
that I am under no obligation to purchase any
books as explained on the back of this card.

Scratch Here!
then look below to see
what your cards get you...

345 SDL C6KG   **245 SDL C6KC**

NAME   (PLEASE PRINT CLEARLY)

ADDRESS

APT.#   CITY

STATE/PROV.   ZIP/POSTAL CODE

Twenty-one gets you
2 FREE BOOKS and a
FREE MYSTERY GIFT!

Twenty gets you
2 FREE BOOKS!

Nineteen gets you
1 FREE BOOK!

TRY AGAIN!

Visit us online at

www.eHarlequin.com

(S-IM-OS-10/00)   DETACH AND MAIL CARD TODAY!

© 1998 HARLEQUIN ENTERPRISES LTD.® and TM are
trademarks owned by Harlequin Books S.A. used under license.

The Silhouette Reader Service™ — Here's how it works:

Accepting your 2 free books and gift places you under no obligation to buy anything. You may keep the books and gift and return the shipping statement marked "cancel." If you do not cancel, about a month later we'll send you 6 additional novels and bill you just $3.80 each in the U.S., or $4.21 each in Canada, plus 25¢ shipping & handling per book and applicable taxes if any.* That's the complete price and — compared to cover prices of $4.50 each in the U.S. and $5.25 each in Canada — it's quite a bargain! You may cancel at any time, but if you choose to continue, every month we'll send you 6 more books, which you may either purchase at the discount price or return to us and cancel your subscription.

*Terms and prices subject to change without notice. Sales tax applicable in N.Y. Canadian residents will be charged applicable provincial taxes and GST.

If offer card is missing write to: Silhouette Reader Service, 3010 Walden Ave., P.O. Box 1867, Buffalo NY 14240-1867

BUSINESS REPLY MAIL
FIRST-CLASS MAIL   PERMIT NO. 717   BUFFALO, NY

POSTAGE WILL BE PAID BY ADDRESSEE

SILHOUETTE READER SERVICE
3010 WALDEN AVE
PO BOX 1867
BUFFALO NY 14240-9952

NO POSTAGE
NECESSARY
IF MAILED
IN THE
UNITED STATES

"I refuse to believe that."

Tom sighed. "I appreciate your support, Tina, more than you know. But all the evidence is pointing toward my involvement in something shady. Why else would I have a falsified driver's license? Why would I have given the post office the wrong address for my box?"

"There is more than one explanation," she said firmly. "I'm sure of it."

"And what would that be?"

"I'm not sure, but I know there is one."

Tom pushed her hair off her face, and Tina thought his hand trembled. "You're too good to get involved in something ugly. And I have a feeling that's what's going to happen. I've loved spending time with you, loved every minute we've spent together, but maybe it would be better if you stayed away from me."

No! She wouldn't let that happen, Tina thought stubbornly. "Better for whom? For me?"

"Of course."

"I don't think so." She was struck by a sudden fear. "Would it be better for you?" she asked in a small voice.

"Of course not. How can you even think that?"

"Then there's no problem. You'll just have to get over your noble offer."

Tom touched her cheek. "It might be best."

"It wouldn't be," she said firmly. "The only way you're getting rid of me is if you don't want to see me anymore."

She held her breath as he slowly shook his head. "You know that's not true."

"Then it's settled." Tina let her breath out and

reached for his hand. After a moment he took it, then twined their fingers together.

"Thank you," he said in a low voice. "Your trust is a gift more precious than anything I could ask for. I won't do anything to betray it."

She knew he wouldn't. And her certainty worried her. She had spent her life avoiding relationships with men. Watching her parents, she had only seen the ugliness of marriage, the broken trust and shattered dreams. She had always vowed that she would never put herself in that position, never allow herself to be controlled by a man, or by her desire for a man.

But her feelings about Tom were too strong to be denied. She tried telling herself that it was the novelty of the situation, the fact that he needed her help. But deep down, she had to admit that she was obsessed with the man. Even at work, she found herself thinking about him. And that both frightened and thrilled her.

"I know you won't betray my trust." Overwhelmed by the step she was taking, she slipped her hand out of his. She might be edging toward getting involved with Tom, but she was determined to be careful. Trying to change the subject, she said, "And now I think it's time we got you home. You're looking a little tired."

"Could we do one more thing first?"

"Of course," she said immediately. *So much for trying to be careful,* she thought wryly. "What do you need?"

"I need a car. Could you take me to a car rental agency?"

She didn't say a thing for a moment. Maybe she had misunderstood. Maybe he wasn't as interested in spending more time together as she had thought. If he had a car, he wouldn't need her to drive him around. He would be independent.

"Are you sure you should be driving?" she finally said. She was fishing, trying to figure out why he wanted a car, and she hated it. She wasn't going to play games, she told herself fiercely.

But before she could tell him not to answer, he took her hand again. "Maybe I shouldn't be. But I was frantic last night, worrying about you. All I could think was that if you needed me, I had no way of getting to you. So I have to have a car. And I don't care if I'm not supposed to be driving yet."

Her face burned. "I suppose it won't do any good to tell you that I can take care of myself?"

"Not a bit of good," he said firmly. "I won't change my mind."

"All right."

They got into her car and in a few minutes they pulled up outside the office of a car rental agency. "Do you want me to come in with you?" she asked.

"Thank you." He gave her a grateful look. "Doing business is still somewhat disorienting. It'll help if you're there."

Twenty minutes later they stood next to a black Ford Explorer. "You were pretty determined to get this car," she said.

"As soon as I saw it, I felt like it was the car I should be driving."

"Then maybe it is." She stood to the side and watched him swing into the driver's seat. "You look like you're familiar with the car."

"It feels familiar. But I wasn't driving this kind of car when I had the accident, was I?"

She shook her head. "It was a sedan of some sort."

He gripped the wheel and stared out the window, and suddenly she saw his uncertainty. "Do you want me to ride with you for a while, at least until you're certain you're comfortable driving?"

"I would appreciate that, but I'm not sure you want to take that kind of risk." He gave her a smile, but there was no humor in his eyes. "After all, the last time I was in a car, I ended up in an accident."

"I'll take my chances," she said. "If I don't like the way you're driving, I'll take over."

"It's a deal."

Tom started the engine and pulled out of the parking lot, driving carefully. It was just one more reason to believe he was a good man, she told herself. His main concern had been for her. He hadn't wanted her to take the risk of driving with him. No, there was nothing shady about Tom Flynt. He was a good man, and she refused to believe any differently.

But she intended to be very cautious. She wasn't about to jump into anything and make a mistake, the way her mother had. She might enjoy Tom's company, and she might want to spend time with him, but she would go slowly and cautiously. Tom was a strong man, and she wanted to be sure that strength didn't translate into dominance and control.

"How does it feel?" she asked, forcing herself to concentrate on Tom's driving.

"Pretty good." He glanced over at her and gave her a thumb's up. "I definitely feel like I'm familiar with this kind of car."

"Why don't we head back to the rental agency, then? I'll follow you home, and you can take it easy for a while. We've done an awful lot today."

"All right. But I'm going to follow you home instead."

"It's the middle of the day," she said, laughing. "What do you think could happen?"

"I don't know, Tina." He was very serious. "But the more we drive around this town, the more tense I am. I don't know why, but I'll feel better if I check your house."

"All right." He looked so serious and concerned that a frisson of fear shot through her. "That's fine with me."

A half hour later, he had checked her house thoroughly, inside and out. Finally he said, "Everything looks fine."

"Thank you."

He nodded. "I'll talk to you later tonight," he said, giving her a strained smile. "I think I'm going to take a nap."

She took a deep breath and said, "I enjoyed spending the day with you, Tom."

"Me, too." He leaned over and brushed her cheek with his lips, turned and got into his car. "So long, Tina."

"Goodbye," she murmured as he drove away. She watched until his car disappeared, then she went inside, being careful to lock the door behind her. Tom's anxiety on her behalf was spooking her, she told herself disgustedly. Grand Springs was a safe town, and there hadn't been anyone outside her house the other night.

But two nights later, she woke from a sound sleep and sat bolt upright in bed. She held her breath, but heard nothing but the familiar silence of her house at night. She closed her eyes and lay back down, telling herself she'd merely been dreaming.

Then she heard the noise. It sounded like someone was scratching at the back door. Her heart pounding, she reached for the telephone beside her bed, keeping her promise to Tom that she'd call the police if she heard anything else. Then she huddled in bed, straining to listen, wondering if there was someone outside her house.

She heard the sound of a car pulling up to the curb in front of the house, and she ran to the window. It was a patrol car from the Grand Springs Police Department. Trembling with relief, she struggled into her bathrobe and ran down the stairs.

She could see the reflection of the police officer's flashlight through the windows, and she followed his progress around the house. He stopped when he got to the back. She waited for him to move, but he stayed in one place for a long time.

Had he found something out there? Was he even now trying to arrest a prowler?

Forcing her feet to move, she walked through the dark kitchen and stood next to the window. Gathering her courage, she pushed the curtain aside and looked out.

The police officer was shining his flashlight onto the ground. There wasn't anyone else in sight. As she watched, he straightened and started to walk around the house again. She must have moved, because he swiveled and shined the flashlight on her.

Startled, she squinted against the light. The officer nodded to her, motioned toward the front of the house and kept walking.

A few minutes later the doorbell rang. She looked

out the window, saw it was the police officer, and then opened the door. "Thank you for coming, Officer," she said.

"I'm glad you called." He looked around the house. "Everything okay in here?"

"As far as I know. What did you find?"

"There are some footprints in the mud at the back of your house. They're too big to be yours, and they look pretty fresh. I'd say you had a prowler here tonight for sure."

"Oh." She moved backward and sat down abruptly on the couch. She had been so sure that the policeman would tell her it had all been her imagination.

"He's gone now," he continued. "But we'll cruise by here real often tonight, and tomorrow when it's light we'll get someone to look around again."

He paused, and Tina could see reassurance in his eyes. "Chances are it's just kids acting stupid, ma'am. Go on back to bed and don't worry too much."

"Thank you, Officer." She wondered if she should call Tom, and immediately decided against it. There was nothing he could do tonight, and he needed to sleep.

The police officer nodded to her. "Call us if you hear anything more. And we'll see you in the morning."

After lying awake most of the night, Tina finally gave in and called Tom early the next morning. His voice was groggy, but when she told him what had happened, the grogginess disappeared. "Don't open the door to anyone. I'll be right over."

It was barely ten minutes later when she heard his

car pull up at the curb. She waited for him to step onto the porch, then she opened the front door.

He swept her into his arms without a word, holding her tightly. She wrapped her arms around him, leaning against his hard chest, and felt the fear and tension drain out of her.

"Thank you," she said quietly, lifting her head to look at him. "Thank you for coming."

"Why didn't you call me last night?" he asked roughly. "You know I would have come right over."

She managed a shaky smile. "That's why I didn't call. I knew you needed to sleep. But I did call the police."

"Thank God for that. Where are the footprints?"

"Near the back door. I'll show you."

But before she could open the back door, they heard the front doorbell ring again. When she opened the door she was shocked to see Detective Jones at the door. "Detective," she said, "what are you doing here?"

"I came to talk to you. I saw the report about your prowler."

"Oh. The officer last night said that someone would come by in the morning. I didn't realize it would be you."

"One of our evidence guys will be here later. I came because I wanted to talk to you."

"Come in."

Detective Jones stopped dead when he saw Tom come out of the kitchen. "Flynt. I didn't know you were here."

"I called him this morning and asked him to come over."

"I see." The detective's gaze swung from her to

Tom and back again, boring into her. "Have you considered the possibility that Tom Flynt was your prowler?"

"Of course not," she said immediately, instinctively reaching for Tom's hand. "Why would he do something like that?"

"He has some connection to the Steele murders," Jones said. "I just haven't figured out what it is."

"And why would that make him prowl around my house in the middle of the night?"

"Yes, Detective, why would I do that?" Tom asked.

Jones shrugged. "I never claim to understand why criminals do the things they do."

"Tom would have no reason to prowl around my house," she said firmly. "He's welcome here any time."

Jones scowled. "That's not so smart, Ms. White. You don't know anything about him."

Tina raised her chin. "I took care of him for almost a week in the hospital. I think I know quite a bit about him."

Jones snorted. "Maybe not as much as you think. Do you know where he'd been hanging out before his accident?"

"I have no idea."

"Neither do I, Jones. Maybe you'd like to tell me."

Tina glanced over at Tom and was surprised by the steely look in his eyes.

"Glad to," said the detective as they all sat down. "You know anything about a place called Nell's Tavern?"

"Should I?"

"You ought to. I have several witnesses who have seen you there, often, in the last few weeks."

Tom leaned back against the couch, but he didn't take his eyes off the detective. "I may not remember much, but I don't think it's illegal to visit a tavern," he said mildly.

Tina stared at him, disturbed. She knew what kind of reputation Nell's had. Then she looked back at the detective. "He was new in town," she said. "I'm sure he had no idea about Nell's."

"Exactly what kind of place *is* this Nell's?" Tom asked.

"It's where the dregs of Grand Springs spend their time," Jones said bluntly. "If there's trouble brewing in this town, you can usually find out about it at Nell's. There have been more arrests for drug dealing, fighting and assault at that hole than anywhere else in town for the past three years running." He fixed Tom with his piercing gaze again. "It's also the place to go to get information about anything illegal going down in this area."

"I guess I made an unfortunate choice in drinking establishments," Tom murmured.

Jones snorted again. "I don't think so, Flynt. My witnesses tell me you were mighty interested in the Steeles and the Steele ball. You were asking all kinds of questions about it."

"That doesn't mean anything," Tina objected. "He was a stranger in town, and that ball was the biggest event of the fall season. It was in all the papers. Of course he would ask questions about it."

Tom shot her a grateful look and laid a hand on her arm. "How did you find out all of this?" he asked.

"I've been beating the bushes, asking questions. You're our only lead for the Steele murders. The other guy has apparently vanished into thin air." He leaned toward Tom. "This amnesia of yours is really convenient, isn't it? If you really can't remember anything, and I have my doubts, I'm going to ride your tail until you do remember. And when you do, I'm going to be close enough that you can't slip out of town."

Tina expected Tom to object. Instead, he nodded slowly. "Fair enough, Detective. I hope you're wrong about me, but I'm sure the Steeles are pleased at how diligently you're pursuing this case. Let me know if you find any more information." He smiled, but it didn't reach his eyes. "And I promise I won't sneak out of town in the middle of the night."

"See that you don't, Flynt."

The detective seemed slightly taken aback by Tom's answer, Tina thought with satisfaction. Good. Maybe Tom's cooperation would make Jones see that he was wrong about him.

The detective stood up to leave, and Tom stood up, also. "Have you had any luck tracing the gun I had when you found me?"

Jones's lips thinned. "No. The serial number was filed off."

Tina thought she saw a flicker in Tom's eyes, then he shrugged. "That's too bad."

"I guess it is, Flynt." Jones seemed to have recovered his intimidating attitude. "Honest, law-abiding citizens don't file the serial numbers off their guns. They also have permits to carry them."

Tom spread his hands. "I wish I had answers for you, Detective."

"So do I, Flynt." The detective glared at Tom, and Tina could easily read the message in his eyes. *If I did, this case would be closed.*

"I'll be watching you," the detective said, then turned and walked out the door.

Chapter 10

The closing door echoed like a gunshot through Tina's house. Tom listened to it reverberate for what seemed like a long time, then turned to Tina.

"I'm sorry," he said. "I wish you hadn't had to see that."

"I don't mind," she said, and her voice was fierce. "He isn't right, and he's going to be forced to tell you so."

Tom resisted the urge to sweep her into his arms. He hadn't been able to stop himself when she opened the door that morning, but he was determined that it wouldn't happen again. "He doesn't think he's wrong. And he has good reasons for his suspicions."

"I don't care," she said stubbornly. "I don't believe him. And why did he come over here this morning, anyway?"

Tom sighed. "The fact that I spent time talking to petty criminals at that tavern, asking questions about the Steeles, then ended up at the Steele ball, is pretty damning. I'm sure that just confirmed his suspicions, and if I had to guess, I'd say he came here to warn you.'' He gave her a weary smile. ''He was probably surprised as hell when he saw me here.''

''I hope it made him think a little.''

His heart moved in his chest. ''Tina, are you always so protective of people?'' he asked.

''Most people can defend themselves,'' she answered promptly. ''You're completely vulnerable. I don't want to see Detective Jones or anyone else blaming you for something you didn't do, just because you can't remember.''

He closed his eyes. He could hardly bear to look at the faith and trust in Tina's face. It would just about kill him if he disappointed her. ''We'll have to hope I remember soon, then.''

''When you do, Jones will have to eat his words.''

He opened his eyes and laughed. ''It sounds as if you'll enjoy watching.''

''I will.'' She smiled back and tucked her arm in his. ''I know I woke you up. How about some breakfast?''

''That would be great.'' His arm burned where she touched him, and he wanted to bend down and kiss her. Tina led the way into the kitchen, then smiled as she slipped away from him. Was she completely unaware of his reaction to her?

''How about an omelet?'' she asked.

''Sounds good.''

He studied her as she worked, and realized that she *was* unaware of the effect she had on him. She had no idea that all he wanted right now was to wrap her in his arms and carry her off to a bed somewhere.

How did a woman reach her age and still be so damned innocent?

He remembered her reluctance to talk about her father and her family life in general. There were hidden depths to Tina, and he wanted to know all of them. He wanted to know everything about her with a sudden, deep hunger he was sure he'd never experienced before. He couldn't possibly have forgotten this feeling.

In a few moments, she slid two plates on the table, and they began to eat. "This is wonderful," he said.

"Thanks." She grinned at him. "You should at least get fed after having me drag you out of bed at the crack of dawn."

"I'm glad you called," he said. "Promise you'll call if anything else happens."

"I promise." Her smile faded. "I was scared last night," she confessed. "I know I said that nothing happens in Grand Springs, but I guess I was wrong."

"You should have called. I would have come right over."

"I know. And that's why I didn't call. You were exhausted yesterday."

"Do you have to work today?"

She nodded.

"Do you want me to drive you to work, then pick you up? At least you won't be coming home alone."

"Absolutely not. Thank you for offering, but I'll be fine. I'm sure whoever was prowling around the house last night was scared away by the police. The officer said it was probably kids, and I'm sure he was right."

He was certain that it wasn't kids, but he didn't

know why. "Will you call me as soon as you get home tonight? I'll want to know that you're okay."

Her face softened into a smile, and she couldn't tear her eyes away from him. "Of course I'll call."

The sunlight streamed through the window behind her, turning her dark red hair into a halo of fire. Her blue eyes gleamed with laughter. "I think I like having a watchdog."

He wanted to be far more than a watchdog for Tina. But he couldn't allow himself to take what he wanted. Pushing the chair away from the table, he said, "You've probably got a lot of things to do before you go to work. I'll talk to you tonight."

He fled the house before he could show her exactly what he wanted from her.

Tina left the hospital shortly after eleven o'clock, tired and ready for bed. The lack of sleep the previous night had finally caught up to her, and she was exhausted. Pulling her car out of the employee parking lot, she headed for home.

A car swung in behind her. The bright lights in her rearview mirror were an annoyance, so she slowed down and waited for the car to pass her. But the other car slowed down, too.

As she drove along, her eyes flicked to the mirror, but the car stayed where it was. When she found herself looking more frequently, she stepped on the accelerator. The car behind her speeded up, too.

Fear stirred inside her as she watched, and she impulsively turned down a side street. Surely the car would keep going straight.

But the other car turned, too. She squinted in the

mirror, trying to make out the license plate, or at least the type of car, but the headlights were too bright.

She speeded up again and turned another corner, and the car stayed with her. Now thoroughly frightened, she gripped the steering wheel and tried to think what to do.

Drive to the police station.

But it was on the other side of town, much too far away.

Tom.

She would go to Tom.

But what if the person following her had something to do with the Steele murders? What if he had something to do with Tom? What if he were looking for Tom?

She couldn't lead the car to Tom.

She speeded up and crossed an intersection, but the car behind her simply speeded up, too. She looked around frantically, praying to see a police car, but there were few other vehicles in sight. There wasn't much traffic in Grand Springs at this time of night.

Finally she saw a light turning yellow and speeded up again. She ran through the red light, barely avoiding the cars starting through the intersection in the opposite direction. She glanced in the rearview mirror and saw the other car stopped at the light, blocked by the stream of traffic.

"Thank you, God," she whispered, and quickly made a left turn. She continued to drive, making random turns, until she was convinced that she had lost her follower.

What could she do now? She didn't want to go home. The thought of facing an empty house was terrifying. She had time now to go to the police station, but in the end she'd have to do the same thing—go home alone.

Without thinking twice, she turned the car in the direction of Tom's apartment. She would be safe with him.

The windows of his unit were bright with lights, and she remembered that she had promised to call him when she got home. He must be waiting up for her call. After one more look to be sure no one was behind her, she scrambled out of her car and rang his doorbell.

"Tina! What are you doing here?" he asked as he opened the door.

She fell across the threshold and into his arms. "Thank goodness you're here," she said, wrapping her arms around him and holding on tightly.

"What's wrong?" he asked as he bent his head close to hers. She thought that his lips brushed her hair, but she wasn't sure.

"Someone was following me in a car. I finally lost him, but I didn't want to go home just yet."

"Did you call the police?"

She pressed her face against his chest and shook her head. "I don't have a car phone," she said, her voice muffled. "I've never needed one."

"We'll call them now."

Keeping his arm wrapped around her, he led her over to the phone and called in a report. Then he enfolded her in his arms again. "Someone will be right over."

But she could tell the police officer very little. She hadn't gotten the license plate number, and she hadn't been able to tell what kind of car it was. "I thought it was big—maybe a sports utility vehicle of some sort. And it was a dark color.''

''You know anyone with a car like that?'' the officer asked.

Before Tina could answer, Tom spoke up. ''I have a black Ford Explorer.''

The officer looked up from his notebook, interest sharpening in his eyes. ''Were you following her?''

''No. I've been here all evening.''

''Was anyone with you?''

''No, I was alone.''

The police officer looked at them both, speculation in his eyes. Then he snapped the notebook shut. ''We'll keep our eyes open, but without any kind of positive identification, it's going to be tough.''

''I realize that,'' Tina said. ''Thank you for coming out.''

''No problem.'' He started to leave, then turned around at the door. ''Let us know if you see that vehicle again.'' His eyes shifted to Tom, then back to her again. ''Good night.''

Silence hung between them as they listened to the roar of the police car leaving the parking lot. Then Tom turned to her. ''Do you want some coffee or tea, something warm to drink?''

She hadn't realized she was shivering. ''That sounds good. Thanks.''

She thought he was reluctant to let her go, but he put a kettle on the stove, and came back over to her. He steered her to the couch, but he didn't take his arm away once they'd sat down. ''I'm going to give you two choices,'' he said quietly. ''Either you can stay here tonight, or I'm going to stay at your house. But you're not going to be alone.''

Relief flooded through her, quickly followed by a jolt of caution. There was a sharp edge to his voice that set off the alarms in her head. Her father's voice, harsh with orders and commands, echoed in her mind. "You're being very bossy, aren't you?"

"I'm scared as hell," he said bluntly. "Someone was waiting for you at the hospital, Tina. God knows what would have happened if you hadn't spotted him. There's no way I'm going to leave you alone tonight. I wouldn't get any sleep, and I suspect you wouldn't, either."

She couldn't quite meet his eyes. She didn't want him to see the echoes of caution that lingered in her heart, the sharp, sad suspicion that there was more to his offer than kindness. It was the legacy of her father, and although she fought it, she couldn't completely banish it.

But she didn't want to be alone. So she finally said, in a small voice, "Thank you, Tom. I'd like it if you stayed with me."

"Here, or at your house?" he asked, as he stood up to make her some tea. She was grateful for the momentary distance. She needed to compose herself.

"At my house, I think." She wanted to be on familiar ground. That way she would feel like the one in control. That was especially important because she wanted so desperately to lean on someone right now. And she couldn't do that. She knew far too well what happened when you gave a powerful man even a little control over you.

"Fine," he said easily, handing her a cup of steaming tea. "Why don't you relax and drink this while I throw a few things in a bag."

Without waiting for an answer, he walked into the

bedroom. She could hear him rummaging in his drawers, then he moved into the tiny bathroom.

She sipped her tea and told herself she was an idiot. Tom was no more like her father than she was like her mother. He would never hurt her.

But that hard, stubborn grain of doubt remained, impossible to banish. It wasn't going to disappear overnight, just because she wanted it to.

"Ready to go?" Tom said as he emerged from the bathroom carrying a small duffel bag.

She nodded and stood up, placing the empty mug on the counter. "I'm ready."

He hesitated at the door, watching her. "Do you want me to drive you home? We can leave your car here and I'll bring you to get it in the morning."

She shook her head. "No, I'll drive home." Her voice was thin and she heard the tremble in it. "I'll need it to go to work tomorrow." She didn't want to be without her car. She would be putting herself completely in Tom's hands.

She told herself she was being ridiculous, but didn't change her mind. She slipped behind the wheel of her car, gripping the cold steering wheel and watching her breath stream out in the icy stillness of the car. "You're not thinking straight," she muttered, but she didn't get out of her car and get into Tom's. It was illogical and silly, but she wanted to drive her own car home.

She pulled out of the parking lot, checking for Tom's lights behind her. She half expected to see the bright lights of her mystery pursuer fall into line behind Tom as they swung onto the main street, but there were no other cars in sight. She drove home carefully, constantly checking her rearview mirror, but she and Tom were alone on the deserted streets of Grand Springs.

When they reached her house, she parked in the garage and Tom left his vehicle in the driveway. She started to open the door to the house, but Tom took the keys out of her hand. "You wait here," he whispered. "I'll check the house."

"No way! I'm going in there with you."

He turned to her, and she could see a flash of anger in his eyes. "I don't want you to get hurt, Tina."

"And I don't want you to get hurt," she retorted. "You were in a serious car accident not that long ago, and you're not completely healed. Do you think you'd be a match for someone who was waiting inside for me? If I come in with you, at least it'll be two against one."

He stared at her for a moment, and she braced herself for his anger. Instead, he slowly smiled at her. "You don't do what's expected of you, do you?" he asked.

"What's that supposed to mean?"

"It means that I'm supposed to protect you. But here you are, trying to protect me."

"You're injured," she said, her voice defensive. "What's wrong with trying to make sure you don't get hurt again?"

"Nothing," he said, and she thought there was tenderness in his voice. "But something tells me I'm not used to having women protect me."

"Then I guess you'll have to get used to it."

"I don't know about that," he murmured, and she could see the glint of humor in his eyes. "But I will let you come into the house with me. We've been standing out here fighting for long enough that anyone inside the house should be at least three blocks away by now.''

Tom opened the door before she could answer, and they walked into the dark and silent house. She threw on all the lights, and they checked each room carefully. She noticed that Tom always put himself in front of her when they walked into a new room. When they were satisfied they were alone in the house, they headed for the kitchen. Tina carefully kept her eyes away from the back porch, the place the prowler had been a few nights ago.

''Was anything out of place? Do you think anyone's been in the house?'' he asked.

Tina shook her head. ''No, I don't think so.''

''Good. All the windows and doors are locked. Do you want to stay up and talk for a while, or do you want to go to bed?''

Tina realized she was exhausted. And now that Tom was in the house with her, she knew she would be able to sleep. ''I need to sleep, I think. Let me show you the guest room.''

Tom shook his head, and Tina's stomach clenched with sudden nerves. Then he said, ''I'd like to sleep on the couch down here tonight. It'll be easier to hear someone outside, and I won't have as far to go.''

He hadn't planned on sharing her room and her bed. She wasn't sure if the feeling inside her was relief or regret. ''If you hear anything, you call the police,'' she said firmly.

''Of course.'' He gave her an innocent look. ''What else would I do?''

''I don't want you to be a hero, Tom,'' she warned. ''Don't try to catch this guy.''

''I haven't been a hero yet,'' he said, his voice flat.

She watched him for a moment, but she couldn't read anything in his eyes. "We have no idea who is prowling around the house and who tried to follow me tonight. He or she could be dangerous."

"I'll keep that in mind." He turned off the kitchen light, then stood staring out the window. "I don't see anything right now."

Tina went to stand beside him and peer out into the darkness. The bushes in her backyard threw up strange, twisted shadows, and the dying flowers looked sinister and mysterious. She shivered. "My imagination is working overtime."

He slipped an arm around her shoulders. "There's no one out there now," he murmured. "And I've discovered that I'm a light sleeper. I'll wake up if I hear anything unusual."

"How do you know?"

She saw a rueful grin on his face. "Because it's happened every night since I've been out of the hospital. Every cat on the prowl, every car that pulls into the parking lot, wakes me up."

"Thank you for coming over here, then," she said, and all her fears seemed silly and groundless. "Especially since you knew you wouldn't sleep well."

He gave her shoulders a squeeze. "I'd rather sleep poorly here than sleep poorly in that apartment. At least I'll be here if you need me."

She wanted to turn in his arms and tell him that she *did* need him. She wanted to tell him that she didn't want him to sleep on the couch and she didn't want him to sleep in the guest room. But fear stilled her tongue and kept her silent. She hesitated too long, and the moment passed. Tom let her go and moved to the front of the house.

He moved the curtain aside to look toward the street, and Tina stood at the stairs, cursing her fearfulness and still oddly grateful for it. She wasn't quite ready to take such a big step. "I'll get you some bedding," she said in a low voice, and she hurried up the stairs.

When she returned a few minutes later, Tom was carefully closing all the shades on the first floor. He turned when he heard her coming down the stairs. "I don't want anyone to know I'm sleeping on the couch," he explained. "If someone comes around, I want to surprise him."

"So that you can call the police more quickly, right?" She gave him a pointed look.

"Absolutely."

She laid a pile of sheets, blankets and pillows on the couch. "Here you are. I'll see you in the morning."

She felt him watching her as she walked up the stairs, and she stopped when she reached the top to turn around and look at him.

"Sleep well," he said quietly.

"You, too."

She hurried to her room and closed the door, then leaned against it. She called herself a coward for not kissing him good night, the way she'd wanted to. But she knew what would happen if Tom kissed her back. He wouldn't be sleeping on the couch tonight, and she wasn't sure she was ready for that.

After a restless night, Tina stumbled downstairs far too early the next morning, stopping abruptly on the stairs when she saw Tom sleeping on the couch. He was sprawled on his back, the blanket snarled around his waist. His chest was bare, and she didn't allow herself to look any farther down than that.

She had seen him almost naked in the hospital, but it was a lot different here in her own home. She didn't remember his shoulders being so broad, or his chest being so firmly muscled. The bruising that had colored his left side had faded, and now all she could see was the hardness of his body, his lean strength and power.

She thought she was being perfectly still and silent, but suddenly Tom opened his eyes and stared right at her. She felt the blush start at her neck and suffuse her face with color. "Good morning," she finally managed to say. "I'm sorry. I didn't mean to wake you up."

"No problem," he said easily. He reached for his shirt and pulled it over his head as he sat up. "How did you sleep?"

"Just fine," she lied. "How about you?"

"I didn't hear a thing last night. It was quiet as the proverbial graveyard."

"Good. I was coming down for breakfast," she said, pulling her robe more tightly around herself. "Maybe I'll go take a shower first."

"Go ahead." He lounged back on the couch and watched her. "I'll take a look outside."

"Great." She hurried back to her bedroom and closed the door behind her. Swallowing hard, she realized that her heart was pounding and an unfamiliar need throbbed deep inside her. She had wanted to run down to Tom and throw herself into his arms, she thought, trembling. Instead of retreating to the safety of her bedroom, she'd wanted to toss caution to the winds and leap onto that couch with him. She'd wanted to find out if the rest of him was as naked as his chest.

Chapter 11

Tom watched Tina retreat into her bedroom and cursed himself roundly. He should be thinking of nothing but her safety. But all he could think about was how good she looked in the morning. All he could think about was how she would taste, how she would feel. And how her eyes, still heavy with sleep, would turn hot and needy if he took her into his arms.

With a muttered oath, he swung off the couch and pulled on his jeans. He was the last thing Tina needed to worry about right now. He'd seen the caution in her eyes, the sudden stillness she tried to hide. He wasn't sure why she was so cautious and careful, and he intended to find out. But now wasn't the time.

When Tina came downstairs, almost a half hour later, Tom had checked the outside of her house, brought in her newspaper, and started the coffee. He was sitting at the table with his first cup, reading the paper, when she walked into the kitchen. She stopped in the doorway and stared.

"Good morning," he finally said.

"Good morning." She stared at him for a moment longer, then her mouth curled into a smile. "This looks very domestic."

"Sorry," he said. "I should have waited for you, but I was going to die if I didn't get coffee."

"Don't be sorry," she said, moving into the kitchen and pouring a cup for herself. "I'm glad you made yourself at home." She shook her head and grinned as she sat down across from him. "It's just a little strange, that's all."

He felt a surge of fierce satisfaction. Clearly, she wasn't used to men staying overnight in her house. Trying to smother the triumphant shout that wanted to explode from his chest, he jumped up from the table. "Let me make you breakfast."

"I'm fine," she said, but she didn't look at him. "Sit down and finish your coffee."

They sat together in silence for a while. Tom tried to read the paper, but the words all ran together and he found himself reading each story twice. He was far too aware of Tina, sitting across from him in her nursing uniform. Her scent drifted across the table to surround him, a fresh, clean scent of flowers and the outdoors. Her hair was still damp, but the mass of rich, dark red was already beginning to curl around her face.

His heart pounded and his breath came more quickly. And worst of all, as he watched her across the table, he thought her chest rose and fell more quickly, that her face was flushed with color and her hand trembled on her coffee cup.

When he found himself reaching across the table for her hand, he jumped up and refilled his coffee cup. "What do you have planned for this morning before work?" he asked.

He felt her gaze on his back.

"I promised that I would go in early today," she replied. "That's why I'm wearing my uniform. One of the other nurses is sick, and we're all pitching in to cover her shifts."

He spun around to face her. "How long will you be working today, then?"

"About twelve hours."

"That's a long time," he said, frowning.

She shrugged. "It's only for the one day."

"Does everyone know your schedule?"

"Everyone on my floor does." She set her coffee cup on the table. "What is that supposed to mean?"

He ran his fingers through his hair. "I don't know what it means, Tina, except that your house is going to be empty all day. I don't like the idea of your coming back here alone after being gone so long."

Her face softened. "I'm used to it," she said gently. "This happens every once in a while, and we work the extra hours. Everyone covered for me when my mother was sick."

"I'm not saying that you shouldn't work." He paced around the house again, uneasiness churning inside him. It was more urgent because he didn't know its source. "I'm going to meet you back here when you get off work tonight. Will you call me before you leave the hospital?"

She frowned. "I'm not sure that's necessary."

"I'm not sure either, but will you humor me?"

"Of course." She watched him for a moment, then

stood up. "I've got to get going." She walked over to one of the cabinets and opened a door. "Here's a spare key for the house so you won't have to rush away. You can lock up when you leave."

He stood staring at the key in his hand and his heart turned over in his chest. "You gave me a key to your house."

She raised her eyebrows. "You wouldn't be able to lock the door without it."

"That's not what I mean. You have someone prowling around your house, someone followed you home from work, and you gave me a key. I'm as good as a stranger, Tina. You shouldn't be giving a stranger a key to your house."

She came back to stand close to him. "I trust you, Tom. You're not a stranger. I know you're not the prowler. I know you didn't follow me from the hospital." She gave a shaky laugh. "It's about all I *do* know—that there's no reason not to give you a key."

He couldn't stop himself from reaching for her. He wrapped his arms around her, although his rational self screamed for him to stop. But there was nothing rational about his feelings for Tina. And her gesture of trust overwhelmed him.

He covered her mouth with his and felt her hesitation. He was about to let her go, but she suddenly leaned against him and shuddered. He felt her surrender, felt her mouth tremble and her body become soft and pliant. And need, carefully banked, roared to life inside him.

He tightened his hold on her and she gripped his shoulders. Her head fell back as he kissed her, and he trailed his mouth along her cheek and down her neck. Her scent surrounded him, making him forget everything but Tina.

When she moaned into his mouth he picked her up and carried her to the couch in the living room. She curled her arms around his neck and held on, her mouth still fused to his. And when he laid her gently on the cushions, she pulled him down with her.

He wanted to strip off the white uniform she wore and kiss her everywhere. He ached and burned with need for her. She moved against him, trying to get closer, and his heart leaped with excitement. She wanted him as much as he wanted her.

He swept his hands over her breasts and felt her tense beneath him. "I want to touch you, Tina," he whispered.

She didn't open her eyes to look at him. Instead, she turned her head to find his mouth with hers. "I want you to touch me," she whispered back. Her face filled with a delicate color. "Please."

He groaned and his hands trembled as he unbuttoned her shirt. Beneath her uniform she wore a lacy, delicate bra, and he bent down to kiss her through the material. He heard her gasp, and he moved against her.

He was lost in her, and he didn't care. Nothing existed in the world but Tina and the need she roused in him. He unhooked her bra and touched her breasts, reveling in the satin softness of her skin, the pink of her nipples, and her throaty cries as he suckled her.

His body throbbed, demanding to be joined to hers, to feel every inch of her against every inch of him. When he lifted his head to kiss her again, he felt her panting into his mouth. Groaning again, he slid his hand between them, burrowing beneath her pants and touching the hot, slick core of her.

He felt her startled jerk and the automatic tightening of her legs. Slowly he pulled his hand away from her, her reaction as effective as a bucket of ice water. What was he thinking?

He brushed the hair away from her face and murmured, "I'm sorry, sweetheart."

She opened her eyes and touched his face, and he could see her gathering her courage. "Don't be."

His heart melted. "I should never have started this. And once I did, I shouldn't have gone so far."

She shook her head. "I'm not a delicate flower, Tom."

But she was. He was abruptly convinced of it. And he had no business crushing her innocence. He slid off her and stood up on shaky legs, holding out a hand to help her off the couch. "First of all, it's the wrong place and time. You just told me you have to get to work. And second, you have enough to worry about right now."

She gave him a wistful smile as she rehooked her bra and buttoned her shirt. "I wouldn't call you something to worry about."

"You should." He wasn't going to let her sway him. "Now go on to work. I'll see you when you get home tonight. All right?"

She watched him for a moment, tenderness in her eyes, then she nodded. "All right. And thank you."

Before he could ask her what she was thanking him for, she ran upstairs. Several minutes later she came back down. She came into the kitchen and stopped. "Goodbye," she said, standing by the kitchen door.

He turned and saw the longing in her eyes. It

matched the longing in his heart, but he didn't move. "Goodbye, Tina. I'll see you tonight."

The longing was replaced by tenderness as she nodded. "Tonight."

As Tina drove home that evening, her weariness from a long day at work was overlaid by an edgy anticipation. Tom would be waiting at the house. Her heart raced and her pulse thundered in her ears.

Her cautious nature told her to be careful, to think before she got too involved. But a part of her longed to throw caution to the wind, to forget about the past and live in the present.

Because the present might be all she had with Tom Flynt.

It was a sobering thought, and she tried to keep it in her mind as she turned the corner to her house. But when she saw the lighted windows of her house and knew that Tom was inside, waiting, she couldn't help the trip of her pulse or the excitement that leaped inside her.

And the idea she'd had that morning came back, full-blown. Could she risk it? Should she?

She pulled her car into the driveway behind Tom's car and practically ran to the door. Fumbling with the lock, her hands trembling, she struggled to get it open. Before she could get it unlocked, the door swung open and Tom pulled her into the house.

"Welcome home, Tina."

Her heart trembled as she looked at him, and she wanted to throw herself into his arms. But she had never done anything like that before, and unsure of herself, unsure of what to do, she curled her hands into fists and gave him a shaky smile.

"Hi, Tom. Thanks for being here."

"I told you I would be."

She looked around the house, at the lights shining brightly in the first floor rooms, and blurted, "The house looked so welcoming when I pulled into the driveway. It was a good feeling."

A look of tenderness passed over his face, then he looked away. "I wanted to let you know that everything was okay."

"Thank you."

There was an uncomfortable silence, and Tina told herself fiercely to say something. Anything. "When did you get here?"

"About an hour ago. I wasn't sure when you would get home, and I wanted to have plenty of time to check out the house and the yard."

"And everything was okay?"

"I didn't see a thing out of the ordinary."

"No more footprints?" she asked lightly.

He shook his head. "Nothing."

"Maybe you've scared them away. The police said it was probably kids, anyway."

"Maybe I have." He glanced out the window, and Tina could see the doubt in his eyes.

"But you don't think so," she said quietly.

He looked back at her. "I don't know what to think, Tina. It seems awfully coincidental that you started having prowlers after I came into your life. I have a gut feeling that it has something to do with the Steeles' death."

"But why would anyone be after me?" she asked, frowning. "I don't know anything about it."

"No, but you do know something about me. More than anyone else in this town knows."

"What difference does that make? You don't know any more than I do."

He paced over to the windows and looked outside, then let the curtain drop. "There are way too many things that I don't know."

"Then why worry about it?" she said, grabbing his hand. "I usually have something to eat after I get home from work. Why don't we go into the kitchen?"

Tom looked at her, then looked down at their joined hands. She felt the pressure of his fingers, the heat from his skin, and suddenly wished she hadn't touched him. It had been an impulsive move, done without thinking. Now she was thinking about it way too much.

He brought her hand up to his mouth and kissed her fingers, one by one. She swallowed hard as heat engulfed her. Her hand trembled, and she was sure he could feel it. Then he let her go. "I'd love to sit with you for a while."

Gradually the tension dissipated as they sat at the kitchen table. He asked her about her day, and she found herself telling him the little details, the good and the bad. Finally, she stopped and gave him a rueful smile.

"I'm sorry. After all the time you spent there, you're probably sick of hearing about the hospital. We should talk about something else."

"Not at all," he said, shaking his head. "I'm enjoying it. You obviously love what you do."

"That's no reason to inflict it on you."

But it had felt right, sitting here with the darkness outside surrounding them, telling him the details of her day. It had felt like she'd finally come home, in more ways than one. And she didn't want it to end.

"I should probably get going and let you get to bed. You must be tired."

Tina took a deep breath and clenched her hands in her lap. It was now or never. "I had an idea at work today, Tom," she began.

He had started to stand up, but he leaned forward eagerly. "About what? Did you remember something?"

She couldn't stop herself from reaching across the table, touching his hand. "No, it's nothing about your memory. I'm sorry," she said, watching the hope flicker and die in his eyes.

He shrugged. "It's okay. What is it?"

But she found that she couldn't say it out loud, not with Tom watching her. Her skin was hot and flushed, and her breath caught in her throat. So she jumped up from her chair and paced the kitchen. Taking a deep breath, she said, "It's about your apartment. It's costing you a lot of money to stay there, money we don't know if you have. And since I've had these prowlers, I've been nervous here at night." The words tumbled out in a rush and she couldn't look at him.

"And?" It sounded like he was holding his breath.

Gathering her courage, she turned to face him. "I was wondering if you'd want to move in here. There's plenty of room and it would solve both of our problems. You wouldn't have to pay the rent on that apartment every week, and I wouldn't be alone here."

She was talking too fast and too loud. She gripped the edge of the counter behind her and curled her fingers into the tile. "Think about it, Tom. I'm at work a great deal of the time. We'd hardly see each other if you'd rather be alone."

Tom stared at her for so long that Tina felt herself begin to sweat. He didn't want to stay and didn't know how to tell her so. He thought she was crazy to even think of such a stupid thing. Why would he want to stay in her house?

Then he stood up from the table and came over to her. He pulled her hands from behind her and held them against his chest. "That's the most wonderful gift anyone has ever given me, Tina," he said quietly. "I don't have to regain my memory to know that."

"It's not a big deal. It was just an offer to stay in my house," she protested.

He shook his head, not taking his eyes off her. "It was a lot more than that. It shows me that you trust me enough to let me stay here with you. It shows that you think I can protect you. To someone who doesn't even know what his name is, that's a very big deal."

"I wasn't thinking about that big-picture stuff," she said lightly, feeling her heart pound in her chest. Tom was standing much too close. "I just thought it would be a solution for both of our problems."

"Maybe money isn't a problem for me. What if I regain my memory and we find out that I have millions of dollars stashed away somewhere?" he said, a teasing smile in his eyes.

"Then you can say that you went slumming for a while," she shot back, relaxing a little. "It would be a new experience for you."

His smile faded. "What will your neighbors think?"

"I don't really care. If anyone asks, I'll explain why you're here. They'll understand."

"Will they? I'm not sure I can convince myself that I'm only here for sensible reasons," he mur-

mured. When he looked at her, she saw the need, deep
down in his eyes. It was carefully hidden, but it was
there.

His grip on her hands tightened, and she felt that
slow heating of her blood, that tattoo of her heartbeat
against her chest, that she felt every time she was
close to Tom.

"It might be a big mistake for me to be here with
you, all the time," he whispered.

"No," she said, her voice almost too low to be
heard. "I don't think so."

"Think carefully, Tina. Are you sure this is what
you want?"

"I'm sure." Need stirred inside her, deep down,
unfamiliar and too long denied. "I want you to stay,
Tom."

He watched her for a moment, then nodded slowly.
He let her hands go, but not before kissing them
again, his mouth lingering in her palm. "Then I'll
stay." His eyes flared once, hot with need, then he
added, "In the spare bedroom."

"All right." Her chest felt tight and she was out
of breath. "I'll show you where it is."

She was surprised at the disappointment gnawing
at her as they walked up the stairs. But it was better
this way, she assured herself. She had intended this
to be merely a business proposal. She hadn't been
prepared for the desire that had sparked between them
just now. Which only went to show how naive and
unsophisticated she was.

She stopped at the door to the guest bedroom and
stepped aside. "Here it is," she said, her voice too
bright.

Tom stood in the doorway for a moment, then

turned to her. "It's much more comfortable than the hotel," he finally said. "Thank you."

"It's a fair trade. I won't have to be alone and you won't be spending all your money." She was speaking too fast again.

But he didn't seem to notice. He shoved his hands into his pockets and took a step away from her. "I'll say good night, then, Tina."

The hallway seemed suddenly too small and too narrow. She was far too close to Tom, close enough that she could feel the heat of his body, smell the faint, clean smell of him. "Good night," she said, her heart pounding.

He turned to face her, and she could read the hot spark of need in his eyes. But he merely said, "Get a good night's sleep, and don't worry."

"Thank you," she said. She began to back toward her own room. "There are extra toothbrushes in the closet in the bathroom, and towels, too. Take whatever you need. I'll see you in the morning."

She turned and practically ran to her room, closing the door carefully behind her. She leaned against it for a moment, trembling. What he must be thinking of her! She had made a total fool of herself. And then she'd run to hide in her bedroom.

She needed the night to settle herself. Turning back to the door, she listened carefully and heard Tom downstairs. He was probably turning off the lights and locking the house, she thought with a stab of guilt. She should have done that herself. But she'd been so shaken by what had gone unspoken between them that she'd hidden in her bedroom instead.

And she had no intention of facing Tom again tonight. So while he was downstairs, she slipped into the bathroom. When she finished washing her face, she hurried back to her bedroom and closed the door again. She'd be much better equipped to face Tom in the morning, when she was rested.

Tom waited in the kitchen as he listened to Tina moving around above him. There was no way he was going back up those stairs until she was in her room, with the door shut and the lights out. She hadn't intended to offer him a sexual invitation when she asked him to move in with her. He knew that perfectly well. Tina was too innocent, too inexperienced. He was willing to bet she hadn't even thought of that aspect of her proposal.

But when he looked at her and saw the longing in her eyes, the need that she was too inexperienced to hide, all he'd wanted to do was sweep her into his arms and carry her to bed. It had taken all his strength to step away from her. And when they had stood in the doorway of her guestroom and he saw the awareness in her eyes, he had known it was a mistake for him to stay.

He'd also known he had no choice. If Tina was in danger because of him, he had to stay. And even though sleeping in her house with only a thin wall separating them would be the torture of the damned, he wouldn't leave her alone.

Finally she stopped moving around. He walked to the bottom of the stairs and looked at the closed door to her room. No light escaped from the crack at the bottom of the door. Presumably Tina wouldn't be coming out of her room again tonight. It was safe to go into his.

But as he tossed and turned on the bed, he couldn't

forget Tina's face as they'd stood in the doorway of this room. Need had fought with fear in the deep-blue depths of her eyes. She'd tried to hide the fear, but it was there. And he vowed to find out why.

Chapter 12

After Tina left for work the next day, Tom moved his meager possessions out of the hotel and into Tina's house. Then he sat down in the living room and called the police station. He asked for Stone Richardson, then waited on the line.

A few minutes later he heard, "Richardson here."

"Detective, it's Tom Flynt," he said.

"How're you doing, Flynt?" the detective said. "Have anything new for me?"

"I haven't remembered anything more, if that's what you're asking. I'm calling to tell you that I've moved."

Stone grunted and Tom heard the rustling of paper on the other end of the phone. "Okay. Give me your new address."

Tom repeated Tina's address, and there was dead silence on the line. Finally Stone said carefully, "Isn't that Tina White's address?"

"Yes, it is." Tom tried to keep his voice level and unemotional. "She was concerned about the prowlers that have bothered her, and asked me to move in with her so she'd feel more secure."

"That so?" Tom heard the disbelief in the detective's voice. "I'm not sure how wise that was, Flynt."

He wasn't sure, either. "She didn't feel safe, living here by herself."

"We could have increased the patrols around her house."

"I'm sure she'd appreciate that, but the police can't sit outside her house twenty-four hours a day."

"And she thought it would be safer to have you living in the house?"

Tom knew exactly what Richardson was thinking. Tina had to be nuts to trust him. It was what Tina should have been thinking, too. But she *did* trust him, and he would die himself before he let anything happen to her. "That's what she thought. I didn't call to discuss the propriety of the arrangement, Richardson. I just wanted to make sure you have my most current address."

"Good thing you did." Tom could hear him writing something. "I'll let Detective Jones know, too. He'll want to keep tabs on you."

"Thank you. I'll keep in touch if I remember anything."

"You do that, Flynt."

Tom hung up the phone and stared out the window. Tension hummed down his nerves and a sense of urgency tugged at him. He opened the back door and walked down to the place where the police had found the footprints.

He tried to force himself to focus, to wrestle his

memories back where they belonged. But they stubbornly refused to return. He had no idea what the footprints meant, or who they might have belonged to.

He spent the rest of the day working around Tina's house, trying to make it more secure. He wasn't sure how he knew what to do, but found that if he stopped trying to remember, his fingers flew as if they had their own memory. By the time Tina was due to return home, he was fairly certain no one could get into the house easily and without giving plenty of warning.

His heart leaped when he heard the crunch of her tires on the driveway that night. When she walked in the door, he saw a hesitant expectancy in her eyes that made his pulse trip once, then begin to pound.

"Hi, Tom," she said, and her voice was breathless.

"Hi yourself." He shoved his hands into his pockets. If he hadn't, he would have grabbed her. "How was work?"

"Fine." She clutched her purse in front of her like a shield. "Did you, ah, move your things into the house today?"

"Everything's here. Not that there was much to move."

She nodded just a little too vigorously. "That's good. Did you find everything you needed?"

"It's okay, Tina," he said, walking to her and taking her hands. They were ice cold. "I'm just as nervous about this as you are. Are you having second thoughts?"

She hesitated just a moment, then gave one jerky nod of her head. "Not about you, Tom," she hurried to say. "It's just that I've lived alone since my mother died and I'm not sure how it's going to feel to have someone else in the house with me.''

He shifted her hands so their palms were pressing together. ''I don't know if I'm used to living alone. I think I might be,'' he said thoughtfully. ''It felt right when I was by myself. But I really don't know. So it's going to be new for both of us.'' He pressed her hands gently, then let her go. ''And I want you to know that I intend to stay in my own bedroom.'' He paused, then added in a low voice, ''Unless you have other ideas.''

She looked down at her feet. ''I don't know what I want,'' she murmured, and he could hardly hear her. ''So I guess that would be best.''

His heart moved at the confusion in her face. ''I'm not putting any pressure on you, Tina. As far as I'm concerned, I'm here because you're concerned about the prowler. All right?''

She looked up and nodded. ''All right.''

There was a shadow in her eyes that looked a lot like disappointment, and his heart leaped again. But he had made a promise and he intended to keep it. As much as he wanted to make love with her, he wasn't going to push Tina into bed with him.

''Come on into the kitchen,'' he said, deliberately changing the subject. ''Have something to eat and tell me what happened at the hospital today.''

He caught a glimpse of the clock as they sat down at the kitchen table. ''You're home early tonight, aren't you?''

She shook her head, and he thought there was a faint wash of color on her cheeks. ''No, I just left on time. I usually get caught up with paperwork and end up staying later.''

He wondered if she'd left early because she knew he would be waiting at the house. Squashing the flutter of hope, he said casually, "I'm glad you were able to get away on time."

She seemed to relax as they talked, and he leaned back in his chair, enjoying her animation and the quiet comfort of the evening. He wished he could sit here every evening when she got home from work, talking to her and watching her across the table.

Her eyes sparkling, she asked him what he'd done today. But just as he began to tell her about his move and his conversation with Stone Richardson, he heard a noise outside the window.

Without stopping to think, he raced for the back door. He reached instinctively for something on his left side, but his hand came away empty. Fumbling with the locked door, he burst outside into the night.

A dark figure retreated, running through Tina's yard and disappearing into the shadows behind the garage. He raced after him, but by the time he reached the back of the garage, the intruder had disappeared.

He hesitated for a moment. All of his instincts told him to pursue the prowler. He might be hiding in the shadows in a neighboring yard. But he looked back at the house and saw Tina standing in the door, silhouetted against the light from the kitchen.

Running back to her, he called, "Get into the house and out of the light!"

She moved away from the door, but not far enough. Slamming the door closed, he whirled to face her. "What were you doing in the door like that? You were a perfect target."

"I'm sorry, I wasn't thinking." She stared at him,

her eyes wide pools of fear. "What's wrong, Tom? Why are you looking at me like that?"

The terror he'd felt for her was fading, along with the burst of anger. "I'm sorry, Tina. I shouldn't have yelled at you. But when I turned around and saw you standing there, my heart almost stopped. I was terrified that the prowler would shoot you."

"Oh," she said faintly.

But fear lingered in her eyes. He reached for her hand, and was surprised when she flinched away from him. "Tina?"

She swallowed once, painfully, and he watched the ripple of muscles in her throat. Then she slowly reached for him. "I'm sorry, Tom. I didn't understand." She gripped his hand tightly. "I'll be more careful."

Her hand was cold, and he could feel her trembling in his grip. "You weren't frightened of the prowler, were you?" he asked slowly. "You were scared because I yelled at you."

She shrugged, trying to make it a casual gesture. She didn't succeed. "I guess I have delicate sensibilities," she said lightly. "I'll have to harden up."

He pulled her slowly toward him. When he enveloped her in his arms, he could feel the tension quivering in every muscle of her body. "I'm sorry, sweetheart," he murmured, stroking her back. "I was afraid you would get hurt."

"I know," she mumbled into his shirt. "I was just acting stupid."

But there was more to it than that. Now he was determined to find out everything about Tina. Something had happened to her, and he wanted to know what it was. He wanted to make sure that no one ever hurt her again.

She sighed and relaxed in his arms, and desire swept over him. But he kept it banked. Now wasn't the time. Finally he held her away from him and looked into her eyes. "Are you okay now? I have to call the police."

She nodded. "I'm fine. And I already called them, as soon as I saw you running through the yard."

Once again, he heard tires crunching on her driveway, and a door slammed in the front of the house. "Here they are," he said, and let her go. He wanted to hold onto her, to wrap his arms around her and protect her from whatever demons had frightened her. But she moved away from him toward the door. Reluctantly, he followed her. He wanted to catch whoever was terrorizing her, but right now, Tina herself was more important.

The police stayed for a long time, questioning both of them. Tina became indignant when she realized that the officers were skeptical of Tom's story of an intruder running away. "I saw him, too, Officer," she said to the one taking notes, her voice frosty. "He wasn't a figment of Mr. Flynt's imagination."

The officer nodded, but Tom could see the doubt in his face. Finally he snapped his notebook shut. "We're going to take a look around the house. I'm sure he's long gone, but we'll want to be sure. And we'll patrol the area every half hour or so tonight. Please don't get alarmed if you hear us outside."

"Thank you, Officer." Tina's voice was prim, but Tom saw the fury banked in her eyes. He grabbed her hand when the policemen stood up to leave, and squeezed when she started to say something else.

She gave him a startled look, but by then the policemen were out the door. As soon as it was closed, she spun around to face him.

"They thought you'd made the whole thing up," she said, furious. "I could tell. Why did you stop me from saying something to them?"

"Because it wouldn't have done any good. They would only have figured that you were part of whatever is going on."

"How do you know that?"

How *did* he know that? "I don't know," he said slowly. "I don't know where that came from. But it's true."

The fury disappeared from her eyes as he watched her. "You seem to know an awful lot about law enforcement."

"I think the Grand Springs police have noticed that, too," he said dryly. "And that's why they're so suspicious."

She watched him for a moment, then tucked her hand through his arm. "That's too bad," she said lightly. "They should be spending their time trying to find the man who killed the Steeles instead of suspecting you."

He covered her hand with his, feeling her satiny skin and delicate bones. Tina looked so fragile, but there was steel beneath her soft exterior. The prowler and his own dilemma faded from his mind as he looked down at her. Suddenly, all he wanted was to explore every facet of her, to know everything about her.

"Tina," he murmured, and her eyes darkened as she stared up at him.

"What?" she whispered.

He bent to kiss her, and felt her instantaneous response. Fire leaped in his blood, cutting through the darkness inside him until there was nothing but Tina. He felt himself falling, losing control, and forced himself to open his eyes.

"Tina," he gasped, as he tore himself away from her.

Her eyes fluttered open and he saw her passion there, a passion that he had awakened in her. For a moment of madness, he could think only of kissing her again, of covering her body with his and making her his own. The drumbeat of desire pounded in his blood and in his head, and he drew her closer. Then he closed his eyes and loosened his hold on her.

"We can't," he said, his voice low and tortured. All the reasons why he couldn't touch Tina came roaring back to him. And now there was one more—he was afraid that if he touched her again, he wouldn't ever be able to let her go. And he had no right to make that promise to her.

She didn't move away from him, but he felt her jolt back to reality. "You're right," she said, disappointment lacing her voice like velvet seduction.

He opened his eyes and saw the frustration in her face and bent down to kiss her. "Sweetheart, I don't want to make love with you because you're frightened. When we make love, I want it to be because it's what we both want and need."

She lowered her head so that he couldn't see her eyes anymore. "I know."

He kissed the top of her head. "Go on to bed. I'm going to take another look around the house."

At that, her head flew up and she searched his face. "You'll be careful, won't you?"

"Absolutely." He would be more careful than he ever had in his life. Because if the prowler got past him, Tina was unprotected.

"All right. But I'll be listening for you to come back inside."

"I'm not going to do anything stupid, Tina. Believe me."

Finally, she smiled. "Why do I think we have different definitions of stupid?"

He stroked the side of her face. "Has anyone ever told you that you have a smart mouth?"

"I don't believe so." Her eyes sparkled with humor. It was a more welcome sight than the fear that had been there earlier.

"Consider yourself told."

She grinned and headed toward the stairs. As he watched her walk toward her bedroom, he felt his heart fly from his chest to follow her.

In the next two weeks, Tina found herself hurrying home from work every day. She no longer lingered at the hospital to talk to the other nurses or volunteered to take extra shifts. She still loved her work, but now her focus was on getting home.

Because Tom was there.

He always made sure he was at the house when she got there. She knew he spent a lot of time driving and walking around Grand Springs, trying desperately to remember why he was there. But no matter where he went, he got back to her house before she did.

And every time she pulled into her driveway and saw the lights blazing from the windows, her heart jolted in her chest and her pulse sped up. The lights meant Tom was inside.

The last two weeks had been wonderful, but they'd also been more frustrating than any two weeks she could ever remember. Tom was trying hard to be a gentleman. He tried to avoid touching her. But the house was small, and they couldn't avoid brushing against each other in the hallway, or bumping into each other when they worked in the kitchen. Every touch, however brief, set off tiny explosions inside her. And whenever she looked at him, she saw heat smoldering in his eyes.

If she'd been more brave, or more experienced, she would have kissed him herself. But she wasn't quite sure what to do, or how to go about seducing him. So she waited, aching with need, tossing and turning every night, her sleep disturbed by erotic dreams.

Thanksgiving was approaching, a tiny dark cloud in the brightness of her life with Tom. One evening, after she'd come home from work, he surprised her by asking what was wrong.

"What do you mean?"

"Something is bothering you," he said gently. "Does it have something to do with Thanksgiving?"

Her first impulse was to deny it, but she found herself saying, "Yes, I guess it does."

"Can you tell me?" he asked, taking her hand across the table."

She was surprised to find that she wanted to tell him about it. "This is going to be my first holiday without my mother. I thought I was getting better, but I guess it's bothering me more than I thought it would." She turned her hand and gripped his.

He brought their joined hands up to his mouth. He only touched her, she thought wryly, when there was at least a table separating them. "You won't be alone, you know. I'll be here with you."

"I'd hoped you would be, but I didn't want to assume."

He lifted his head to look at her. "There's nowhere else I'd rather spend Thanksgiving," he said.

"Thank you."

He kissed her hand one more time, then took his hand away and leaned back in his chair. He had been doing that for the past two weeks. Every time he got too close to her, he quickly backed away. "Are we going to make the traditional Thanksgiving dinner, with all the trimmings?"

"Absolutely. And we'll watch the football games, too."

"Football?" His eyes laughed at her. "Are you sure?"

"My mother and I watched the football games every year," she said. "It's part of the tradition."

"Then football it will be."

She didn't let him forget about his promise the next morning. "Get out of bed, sleepyhead," she said, sticking her head inside his door. She kept her gaze firmly fixed on his head. She refused to look at his bare chest or where the blanket dipped dangerously low on his hips. "We have to get to the store. It's the day before Thanksgiving. Do you know how crowded it will get?"

Groaning, he turned to look at her. "I didn't know you were going to be a slave driver about this."

"I'll meet you downstairs in fifteen minutes," she called, and hurried down to start the coffee. She'd been dreading the holiday for months. Now, suddenly, she was looking forward to the ritual of preparing a Thanksgiving meal.

The next afternoon she sank down onto the couch and reached for Tom's hand. "Come sit down. Now all we have to do is wait for the turkey to finish cooking." Already, mouth-watering smells were filling the house.

Instead of sitting down, Tom held her hand for a moment and looked down at her. "You look happy, Tina."

"I am happy." Her heart expanded in her chest. "You've taken a day I've been dreading and made it into something special." He had searched through her recipes and picked out several to try. Then he had teased her and made her laugh while they were getting the meal ready, until she'd been light-headed with delight.

"You deserve to be happy. Holidays have always been special for you, weren't they?"

"How could you tell?"

He smiled. "I can tell a lot of things. Your face is very expressive."

"No one's ever said that before."

"Maybe no one's ever looked closely enough before."

Suddenly, she wanted him to know everything about her. She wanted him always to be able to see into her heart, and know what was there. But her mind, still too cautious, skittered away from the thought.

"Come on and sit down. I think the football game is about to start."

But as they watched the traditional Thanksgiving football game, she felt his gaze on her face more often than it was on the action in front of them. Her heart pounded, banging against her ribs until she was sure he could hear it. Finally she jumped up from the couch.

"I'll go check on the turkey."

But instead of staying in the living room, he followed her into the kitchen. "How does it look?"

He was right behind her, so close that she could smell the faint tang of his scent over the smell of roasting turkey and dressing.

"I think it's about ready," she said breathlessly.

"Mmm, I think so."

She felt his breath on her neck and her skin tingled. When she reached for pot holders to take the turkey out of the oven, he slid them out of her hands. "Let me," he murmured.

She stepped aside, realizing that she was shaking. He quickly removed the turkey, along with the dishes that held the dressing and a casserole they'd made.

In a few moment, they were sitting at the table. Tom's dark eyes were fixed on her as she tried to eat. The food was delicious, but she hardly noticed the taste. She couldn't tear her eyes away from Tom. Her heart was pounding and her palms sweating. Desire rose inside her, blooming into a desperate need that she'd never felt before.

Her hands were shaking by the time they finished eating. They put the food away, then Tom started to do the dishes. Tina touched his arm, feeling his muscles like corded iron beneath his shirt. Apparently, he was as tense as Tina. He was just better at hiding it.

"Don't worry about the dishes," she said, her voice low and husky and unfamiliar. "We can do them later."

He turned to face her, and stilled when he saw her face. "Are you sure?"

"I'm positive."

"Then what do you want to do?"

That was the question. Tina wanted to be courageous and kiss him, but she didn't know how. She was afraid she would be awkward and fumbling and not know what to do. She hesitated, then saw the understanding in Tom's eyes.

It was enough to steady her. "This is what I want to do," she said, and reached out for him.

Chapter 13

She could feel Tom resisting, feel him holding himself back. Then, with a groan, he wrapped his arms around her. He kissed her like a man dying of thirst who has just found water. He kissed her as if he never wanted to let her go.

"Tina," he groaned, "I've been trying so hard to stay away from you. Why did you have to do that?"

"Why were you trying to stay away from me?" she murmured against his mouth.

"Because I was afraid of what would happen if I touched you again. And it shouldn't happen."

It took every bit of courage she possessed to lean back and look at his face. "What were you afraid would happen, Tom?"

He ran his hand along the side of her face and gently eased her hair away from her forehead. "I was afraid that if I touched you again, I wouldn't be able to stop. I was afraid that if I kissed you, I would end up making love to you.''

Her heart leaped in her chest. ''Why would that be wrong?''

''Because you don't know me, Tina. You don't know who I am, and neither do I. It wouldn't be fair to you.''

''Do you think you're married?''

Slowly he shook his head. ''I can't say no. But I don't think so.'' He hesitated, then said, ''I don't think I could feel the way I feel about you if I were married.''

Her throat swelled and her heart melted. ''Then where's the problem?''

''Don't you see? I can't make any promises to you. I don't have the right. You know nothing about me, really.''

''I know everything about you that I need to know. You've been living in my house for more than two weeks, for heaven's sake. I know what kind of person you are.''

His eyes glittered with desire, but she could see the tenderness there, too. ''Are you trying to seduce me, Tina?'' he said, bending forward to kiss her.

''What do you think?''

''I think I hope you are.''

She closed her eyes. ''I think I am.''

''It's working.'' He bent to kiss her again, and her body turned to water. She pressed against him, shaking, and he groaned into her mouth.

Then he swept her into his arms. ''Where do you want me to take you?'' he asked, and she realized that even now, he was giving her a choice. They would make love only if it was what she wanted.

"The bedroom," she whispered, feeling her face flush. She had no idea she could be so bold.

He tensed, then she could feel his body trembling, too. He buried his mouth in her hair, then raised his head. "Are you sure, Tina?"

Slowly she nodded, and suddenly all the fear was gone. This was exactly what she wanted, what she had wanted for a long time. "I want to make love with you," she said.

He carried her up the stairs and into her bedroom. Snow had started falling, and the world outside the windows was bright and silent. The only thing she heard was her breathing, and Tom's. They both sounded as if they'd been running.

Tom lowered her to her bed, and pulled back the quilt. He stood watching her as he unbuttoned his shirt and tossed it aside. Then he pulled off his jeans, until he was dressed only in his white briefs. Tina couldn't tear her eyes away from the huge bulge in the front of them. She swallowed once, hard, wondering if she'd made a mistake.

She began fumbling with the buttons of her own blouse, but Tom took her hands away and kissed them. "Let me. Please," he said.

He knelt in front of her and slowly unhooked each button from her blouse. When he was finished, he pushed it aside and bent to kiss her chest. Her skin jumped and shivered, and she felt her nipples tighten.

Tom noticed, because his eyes darkened and his breathing quickened. Slowly he bent to kiss her breast through the blue silk of her bra. The sensation speared through her and she gasped.

"Have I told you how much I like what you wear under your clothes?" he muttered. His hands swept over her. "But I think I'd like this better if it was someplace else."

He unhooked her bra with one flick of his fingers, then he gently removed it. She was sitting on the bed, naked from the waist up, and she had to squelch an impulse to cross her arms over her chest.

"You're beautiful," he said, smoothing his hands over her. He lifted her breasts in his hands, then bent to kiss each one in turn. Tina forgot about covering herself as she melted with pleasure.

Tom wasn't in a hurry, and by the time he lifted his head, she was whimpering with need. His eyes glittered. "I want more of you, Tina," he said. "May I?"

Wordlessly she nodded. She couldn't have spoken if her life depended on it. Tom pressed her back onto the bed, unfastened her jeans and slid them down her legs. He looked at the tiny scrap of silk that she wore beneath her jeans, then looked up at her face.

"It's a good thing I never saw this," he muttered, "or we would have been in this bed long before today."

Sitting on the bed, he bent and kissed her abdomen, close to the waistband of her panties. As his mouth trailed liquid fire over her skin, he reached up and touched her nipple again. She felt herself lifting off the bed, trying to get closer to him.

In a haze of sensuality, she felt him slip his hand under the lace and cup her intimately.

Before she could react, he slid one finger against her, and a flood of new sensations crashed through her.

With an inarticulate murmur, she pulled him against her. He pressed her against the bed, and she could feel his heat and hardness against her. But before she could panic, he touched her again, and she melted against his hand.

His mouth was on hers, tasting her, kissing her with a desperation she was just beginning to understand. Finally, he lifted his head. ''Don't move, sweetheart.''

He leaned down and grabbed his jeans, fumbling in his pocket. Then he shucked off his briefs and tore open a small foil packet.

''I didn't even think of protection,'' she gasped.

''I did.''

He slid the scrap of lace that was her last covering down her legs and tossed it on the floor. Then he looked at her. His gaze swept her from head to toe, and when he looked at her face again, she saw the tension in the tight lines of his face.

''You're so beautiful, Tina. Inside and out. I've dreamed about this since the first time I opened my eyes and saw you.''

She pulled him down to kiss her again, and as he touched her, she felt the tension coiling inside of her. When she moved against his hand, he slid on top of her.

He moved again, and she felt him probing against her. He slid inside her, then stopped abruptly.

He eased away from her and touched her again. She gasped at the feelings gathering inside her. Then he moved his hand over her and the sensation exploded inside, shattering her. She heard herself calling his name, reaching for him, and suddenly he was inside her.

There was pain, but only for a moment. Then Tom

moved inside her and the sensation began building again.

She shattered again and felt Tom tense around her. Then he shuddered and whispered her name. He wrapped his arms around her and held her tightly.

It took a long time for her breathing to return to normal. She was aware of Tom, pressing her into the bed, his heart beating against hers. Finally he lifted his head.

"Why didn't you tell me?"

"I was afraid you would stop, and I didn't want you to stop."

"Of course I would have stopped. You were a virgin, Tina. You gave me a gift I don't deserve."

"I wanted to make love with you, Tom."

"I'm incredibly honored." He smoothed her hair away from her face. "And I hope I didn't hurt you too much."

She shook her head, a lump forming in her throat at the tenderness in his eyes. "No." She would never forget the care he had taken with her.

"I should have been more careful."

"I'm not a delicate flower, Tom."

"No, but you were a virgin."

"Well, I'm not anymore, am I?" Tina raised herself on one elbow, feeling incredibly sexy. She would never have imagined herself being playful in bed with a man.

Tom watched her for a moment, then he smiled. She saw desire blooming in his eyes again, and felt him stirring against her. "No, you're not, are you?"

Tina opened her eyes and saw that she was pressed against Tom's chest. Her legs were tangled with his, and Tom's hand was curled around her breast.

Memories of the night before flooded her, and she moved against him. But when he opened his eyes and gave her a lazy smile, she had a moment of panic.

What was she supposed to do this morning? As wonderful as last night was, she had no idea how to act in the light of day. She scrambled for something to say, then Tom pulled her close.

"Good morning," he murmured into her ear. "I had a wonderful night. How about you?"

"It was pretty fabulous," she said, unable to meet his eyes.

He sat up in the bed and pulled her with him, arranging the sheet so she was covered. "This has been a day of firsts for you, hasn't it?" he said, kissing her. "And this is your first morning after."

"I wasn't sure what to say," she confessed.

"I know. But it's just me. Remember?"

And suddenly it was all right. This was Tom. The man she…

Her mind stopped. Surely she wasn't ready to say that. Was she? She grabbed the sheet and prepared to bolt out of the bed. She would take a shower and get dressed. Then she could sort out her feelings.

But Tom took her hand. "There is something I wanted to ask you," he said, and she tensed. What would she say if he asked her if she loved him?

"What?"

He reached out and rubbed her back. "I want to know everything about you, Tina. I want to know *you*." He turned her so she was facing him. "Will you tell me about your childhood? About what happened?"

She stared at him for a moment, then relaxed. This was an easier question than the one she'd been expecting. And suddenly she realized that she wanted to tell him. She wanted him to know everything about her. She wanted to be sure that he wouldn't turn away in disgust when he heard where she came from. And what she had done.

"It's a common story, and an ugly one," she said quietly. "My father drank, and he beat my mother."

Tom's hand tightened on hers. "Did he beat you, too?"

"No, my mother protected me. No matter what, she wouldn't let my father touch me. She took a lot of blows that were meant for me."

"No wonder you were so close to her," he murmured.

"I would have done anything for my mother."

"How did your father die?"

She didn't say anything for a long time. Finally she looked down at their joined hands and said, "I killed him."

"What?"

She looked up and saw the shock on his face. "Oh, I didn't shoot him or stab him or anything like that. He was killed in a car accident. But it was my fault."

"How can that be?"

The memories stirred, memories she'd tried hard to suppress. Maybe it was time to bring them into the light of day. "He came home one night, drunk," she said quietly. The scene was suddenly as vivid as the day it had happened. "He was in a bad mood. I could tell, because he was shouting and swearing. I knew he was going to hit my mother again. I was twelve, and something inside me snapped. I locked and barred the doors, and refused to let him in. My mother tried to pull me away, but I was too strong for her. He was screaming about what he was going to do to us, that he was going to get his gun and kill us, and I was afraid. After a while, my father got into his car and drove away. I heard the tires screech as he went around the corner.

"That was the last time we saw him. The police came by an hour later to tell us that he'd been in a car accident. He'd skidded off the road and hit a tree and was thrown out of the car. He was killed instantly."

She looked up at him defiantly. "I was glad, Tom, glad he was dead."

Tom drew her close. "And you've felt guilty about it ever since."

She nodded against him. "I didn't feel guilty because I wouldn't let him into the house. But I was guilty about my feelings afterward. He was my father. How could I be glad he was dead?"

"He might have been your father, but he was a monster. It was natural to be glad he wasn't going to hit your mother anymore."

"I didn't want to have anything to do with men after that. I didn't date at all in high school."

"Who could blame you?" He stroked her face again and leaned back to look at her. "Did you ever get any counseling?"

She nodded. "Once I got into nursing school, I realized I would have to deal with what had happened. I think I have, mostly, but I still have my moments."

"No wonder you were alarmed when I yelled at you."

"That was foolish of me. I guess it was just an automatic reaction."

"It was a natural reaction." He bent down and kissed her again. "I can't promise that I'll never be angry with you, you know."

"I know that. I'm old enough to realize that everyone is angry once in a while."

"You know we'll have our share of fights. All couples do. But I'll never hurt you. I can promise you that."

Her heart soared at his words. He was talking about them as a couple, about a future they might share.

But her fears hadn't completely vanished. Her heart told her that she had nothing to fear from Tom, but years of caution warned her to go slowly.

"I know you'll never hurt me," she said. "But I've spent a long time being cautious. I'm afraid that my old fears may come back to haunt me."

"I understand," he said. "You can't change yourself overnight. But I'm glad you told me what happened. I'll try to be careful."

"No, I'll put my fears aside," she said. "I don't want you walking around on eggshells all the time."

"I don't think I want to spend much time walking in the near future," he murmured. "I much prefer lying down. With you."

He pulled her to him again, and Tina felt passion bloom inside her once more. She reached for him and pulled him close, desperation fueling both of them. Unspoken in their hearts was the fear of what would happen when Tom got his memory back. Would they be able to be together? Or would Tom have to leave?

They made love urgently, desperately, their bodies speaking without words. Tina put all she felt into her lovemaking, until both of them were sated and bone-less on the bed.

Finally Tom rolled over and kissed her once more. "I think we need food," he said.

Tina realized that the sky was already darkening. They had spent the whole day in bed together. Feeling deliciously decadent, she curled her arms around his neck and said, "How about some leftover turkey?"

"Sounds great. For some reason, I couldn't con-centrate on my meal last night."

She grinned at him. "Me neither."

They laughed and teased as they got dressed and went downstairs. Moonlight glinted off the fresh snow in the backyard as they cleaned the kitchen, touching and kissing whenever they passed each other. Finally they sat down to eat cold turkey sandwiches, their fingers entwined.

"I may not remember anything, but I know this much. This was the best Thanksgiving I've ever had," Tom murmured.

Tina squeezed his hand. "I was dreading this hol-iday so much. Now I'll always remember it."

Tom watched her from across the table, tenderness and some other emotion she was afraid to name glow-ing in his eyes. "Our first Thanksgiving together. It will always be a Thanksgiving to remember."

He brought her hand to his mouth and kissed each of her fingers. Desire stirred again, deep inside her, as she watched him.

His eyes darkened as they met hers. "I think we've been up far too long. We need to go back to bed."

"Yes," she whispered, passion swirling inside her. She was amazed she could want him so badly.

He drew her to her feet, reached across the table

and kissed her. She tasted the need he could barely control and leaned back, awed that she could evoke such need. "I've never felt this way before, Tom."

"I haven't either, Tina. I have no doubt of that."

He took her hand to lead her back upstairs, but a shadow moved across the window and she jerked her head around. There was a silhouette, in the shape of a man, against the window.

"Tom," she whispered, her passion instantly replaced by fear.

He spun around and saw the shadow. Without a word, he lunged across the kitchen toward the back door. Just as he reached for the doorknob, he slipped on a throw rug and fell heavily, banging his head against the counter as he went down.

"Tom!" she cried, pushing the chairs aside to get to him, fear swallowing her whole. He lay on the floor, unmoving. "Tom, can you hear me?"

She ran her fingers through his hair. He wasn't bleeding, although he had a small lump on the left side of his head. Grabbing a towel, she folded it over and slipped it under his head.

"Tom." She waited until she could force the panic out of her voice. "Tom, can you hear me?" She thought she sounded very cool, considering she was screaming inside.

Groggily, he opened his eyes and looked up at her. "Tina? What happened?"

"You slipped on the rug and hit your head again. Are you all right? Do you remember what happened?"

He stared at her for a moment, then she saw his pupils dilate. "Tina," he gasped, "help me get up."

"You need to stay where you are for a moment. I want to make sure you haven't reinjured yourself."

"I can't." He struggled to sit up. "I have to get up, and make some phone calls.

"Tina, I've remembered everything."

Chapter 14

Tom stared at Tina, a thousand disjointed thoughts running through his head at the same time. He was dizzy and his head ached with a dull pain, but he ignored it. He remembered!

"What do you remember, Tom?" Tina asked, gripping his hand.

"Everything, I think. I know why I was in Grand Springs, and what I was supposed to be doing here." He raised himself on his elbow and looked around the kitchen. "I need the telephone, Tina. Hurry!"

He could see the fear in her eyes and longed to reassure her. But there wasn't time. He took the phone out of her hand, quickly dialed the police department, and asked for Stone Richardson.

He eased himself into a sitting position against her kitchen cabinets and gripped her hand in his as he waited. Finally Stone came on the line. "Richardson here."

"This is Tom Flynt, and I've remembered everything. I don't have time to explain," Tom said rapidly. "Just listen. You are looking for a black truck, with a Missouri license number." He rattled it off. "It's registered to a Randy Wade. He's the man who killed the Steeles."

Stone started barking questions at him, but he cut him off. "Just put out a bulletin on Wade and his truck, then get over to Tina's house. I'll tell you everything."

Tom turned the phone off while Stone was still sputtering and set it on the floor. Then he turned to Tina and squeezed her hand. "I'm sorry, Tina. You deserve an explanation, but I had to give Stone that information. It's crucial."

"What's going on?" she asked softly. He could see the fear lingering in her eyes. "What have you remembered?"

"Who I am," he answered simply. "Tom Flint is my real name. I just spell it with an 'i' instead of a 'y.'" He gave her a quick smile. "So you're not going to have to get used to another one."

Some of the fear in her eyes melted, but she gripped his hand more tightly. "What else did you remember?"

He pushed himself off the floor and stood swaying for a moment. His head ached, and the room felt like it was twirling around him, but he gathered Tina close. "I'm not a criminal or a fugitive," he said. "I'm an FBI agent. I was here in Grand Springs, undercover, chasing the man who killed the Steeles. That's why I was in Nell's Tavern, that's why I thought I was a good liar. And that's why I knew so much about law enforcement."

"What?" She leaned back and stared at him, disbelief in her face. "I never imagined you were an FBI agent."

"It didn't occur to Richardson and Jones, either," he said dryly. "I guess the Bureau did too good of a job on my undercover ID."

"Tell me everything." She eased him into a chair, then pulled another one next to it. Then she took his hand and held on tightly. He returned the pressure of her fingers. She was his one certainty in a world that was again spinning on its axis.

"I've been following Randy Wade for months. He's a suspect in a string of bank robberies, including one in which he shot and killed two people. Wade is violently antigovernment, and we suspect that he stole the money to bankroll a militia he's trying to form."

"How did you know he would be in Grand Springs?"

"A tip from an informant." He paused, trying to organize the memories that were flooding back. "I was spending time in Nell's because I knew it was the kind of place that Wade would hang around. I was pretty vague about my job, and Nell's is the kind of place where no one questions you too closely." He grinned at her. "It's amazing what a few drinks can do to loosen the tongue. When I started buying, the men in Nell's fell all over themselves to tell me everything they knew about Wade and the Steeles."

"So that's why you spent so much time there?" Tina said slowly.

He nodded. "Wade never could keep his mouth shut. That's why I was able to track him to Grand Springs. I talked to the same men he'd been chatting up at Nell's. They told me that David Steele, Jonathan

Steele's half brother, was bad news and that Wade was real interested in that fact. There were rumors that David had stolen a lot of money from Steele Enterprises. I also found out about the ball, and that Wade had been asking a lot of questions about it. No one knew if anything was going to happen there, but there were more wild rumors—that David and Lisa Steele were going to run away with the money they'd stolen, that David Steele was going to kill his brother. Not a lot of solid information, but enough that I decided to go and keep an eye on David and Lisa Steele. I knew Wade needed money, and the Steeles sounded like troublemakers. I wondered if Wade had offered to help David with some crime in exchange for some of the money David and Lisa stole.''

"Had he?" Tina watched him, still holding onto his hand.

"I don't think so. I think Wade had heard David and Lisa might have a bag full of money, spotted the Steeles running away from the ball with the money, and shot them. He took off, probably figuring that he could make a clean getaway in the confusion."

"And you ran after him."

"I had been watching the Steeles all evening. I saw them put money in a duffel bag and knew it had to be the money they'd stolen. Then the lights went off and they started to run, I ran after them, but I was too late. I saw Wade shoot them and grab the bag David was holding. Then I saw Wade drive away."

"So you followed him."

"It was the only thing I could do. I didn't have time to stop and call the police. Wade would have disappeared. And because I was supposed to be a salesman, I didn't have a police radio in my car. I was driving too fast to take a chance and use my cell phone.''

"How did you end up in that accident?"

"Wade spotted me trailing him. He was cleverer than I gave him credit for. He pulled off on a side road, and when I went speeding past him, he came out after me. He rammed my car until I went off the road. He probably hoped that the accident killed me.'' He gave her a grim look. "But my having amnesia gave him a second chance. As long as I didn't remember anything, he was home free.''

"Where do you think he is now?"

"I have no idea. But I wouldn't be surprised if he's still somewhere near Grand Springs. And I'm betting that he's your prowler.''

"Why would he be hanging around my house?"

"The papers have talked about me, and the fact that you were my nurse. I've seen the articles. He was probably hoping for an opportunity to kill me.''

"What happens next?" Tina asked quietly.

"If he's still here in Grand Springs, we try to catch him.'' He looked out the window at the darkness. "Stone Richardson is a good detective. He'll help me. And Bob Jones will do a good job, too.''

"Are you sure you can convince Detective Jones you're not a criminal?"

Tom looked over at her and flashed her a quick smile. "He'll be convinced. And he's such a bulldog that he won't let go of any leads about Wade. He'll do a good job.''

"You're very forgiving,'' she said.

His smile faded. "Jones was just doing his job. And it looked bad. I would have probably thought the same thing, in his position.''

"They'll be here soon," she said, and he saw the pain in her eyes.

"When they do, I'll have to go," he answered, swiveling in his chair to face her. "It's my job, Tina."

"I know," she said, and she tried to smile. "I understand."

"I'll be back, though. I can promise you that."

"Can you?" she murmured. "You've remembered your job. What about your family?"

Suddenly, he realized what had put that pain in her eyes. "I'm not married," he said cheerfully. "Not engaged or in a serious relationship. In fact, my girlfriend dumped me just before I came to Grand Springs."

Her eyebrows came together. "That must have hurt," she said, watching him carefully.

He shrugged. "Not really. We wanted different things out of life. I'm an attorney, and she wanted me to quit the FBI and open up a law practice. She wanted the glory and the money associated with being a lawyer's wife. But all I want is to be part of the Bureau. I'm happy as an agent and have no intention of quitting. When she realized I was serious, she said goodbye. By that time, I was glad to see her go."

Tom watched Tina digest that news. Then she said, "Do you have a family?"

"A huge one," he said. "Two parents and four siblings. My dad is a cop, and that's why I joined the Bureau. I went to law school because I thought it would give me an edge when I applied. Law enforcement is all I've ever wanted to do."

"Where do they all live?"

"Most of them live in Chicago and the suburbs around it. My dad is a Chicago cop."

"Oh," she said faintly.

"You'll love them," he said, leaning over to kiss her. "And they'll love you."

But he could see the hesitation in her eyes, the doubt. All he wanted to do was take her in his arms and reassure her, tell her that nothing had changed. Then he heard the cars pull up in the street in front of her house, and he knew that everything was going to change.

"Tina, we need to talk," he said, his voice urgent, "but I have to help catch Wade. Promise me you won't worry. About anything."

He stared at her, and she glanced away. "How can I promise that?" she said quietly. "You're going out to capture a dangerous criminal, and you've just been knocked on the head again."

"Don't worry about us, then. Can you promise that?"

She gave him a strained smile. "We'll talk when you have more time, all right?"

He wanted to press her for her promise, but the doorbell rang and he knew he'd run out of time. Frustrated, he ran his hand through his hair as he stood up. "Tina, nothing has changed."

"Yes, it has," she said. "But you don't have time to discuss it." She smiled at him. "I'm not going anywhere, Tom. I'll be here whenever you finish."

It would have to be enough for now. He nodded once, then turned to open the door.

Tina watched Tom as Stone Richardson and Bob Jones walked into her house. He didn't think anything had changed, but he couldn't be farther from the truth.

Everything had changed, and once he had time to think about it, he'd realize it, too.

Tom was an FBI agent. He had a job and a family a thousand miles away. He was in Grand Springs only because of his job, and once it was over, he'd be leaving. Would there be any place in his life for her?

They had become very close in the last few weeks. But as Tina watched him talking to the two detectives, watched him taking charge of the case and giving orders, she realized that she really didn't know Tom at all. She knew he was a good man, kind and caring, but she had never seen him like this.

Her heart felt like it was breaking, and she turned away. Tom had been right. He'd warned her not to get involved with him, told her that he didn't know who he was. He wasn't a criminal, but he sure wasn't an ordinary joe, either.

She was happy he'd regained his memory. His face had softened and his eyes had warmed when he'd talked about his parents and brothers and sisters. They were important to him, and she was glad he had them back. And listening to him now with the two detectives, she realized how good he was at his job.

"The truck is registered to Wade, all right," Richardson had said. "We've got a bulletin out on it, so we'll have to see if anything turns up."

"I called the FBI, and they confirmed you were one of their men." Bob Jones held out his hand. "Sorry I suspected you."

Tom shook his hand vigorously. "You did the right thing, Jones. I would have suspected me, too. You did some nice police work."

Tina thought the tough detective actually blushed.

"What do we do now?" he asked.

"We need to canvas the town, see if anyone has seen Wade," said Tom. "If he's staying around here, he has to eat."

"When I called the FBI, they knew who you were chasing. They're going to fax us a picture of Wade, then follow up with delivery of several more in the morning. We'll start by checking at all the restaurants and the grocery stores to see if anyone can identify him."

"Good." Tom nodded, and Tina thought she saw him wince. "Let's not waste any time. We should get started right now."

"Let's go, then," Richardson said.

Tom turned to her. "Will you be all right here by yourself?"

"I'll be fine." Her heart would be breaking, but she wasn't about to tell Tom. "I'll lock all the doors and windows."

"I don't know when I'll be back. If we get some information, it could be a while."

"Don't worry about it," she forced herself to say. "I have to work tomorrow, anyway."

Tom broke away from the other two detectives and came over to her. "Don't take any chances," he said in a low voice, cupping her face in his hands. "Go to work, come home, and don't open the door to anyone."

"I'll be fine, Tom," she said. She smiled at him, although it was an effort. "You have enough to worry about. You don't need to worry about me, too."

"I'll try not to. But I'll be thinking about you."

He kissed her deeply, and she couldn't stop herself from melting into him. Finally, too soon, Tom broke away. "I'll be back as soon as I can," he said, his voice husky.

"I'll be here." Her hands dropped away from him and she watched him walk out the door with the other two detectives. When they shut the door, she hurried over to lock it behind them. Then she checked all the other doors and windows. When she was sure everything was locked, she stood in the kitchen, her heart full of pain.

Of course, she was glad that Tom had gotten his memory back, that he was no longer under a cloud of suspicion. How could she feel otherwise? But her heart splintered when she thought about the future. Did they have a future together? She wasn't sure.

It wouldn't be fair to hold Tom to any promises he'd made before he regained his memory. And to be fair, he'd never really made any promises in the first place. She was the one who had imagined that they'd have a life together.

But just because it was what she wanted didn't mean it was what Tom wanted. She didn't know him at all anymore. She swallowed a sob and drifted into the living room, sinking down onto the couch. All she could do was wait until this job was completed, until Randy Wade was caught. Then, maybe they could talk about the future.

It was humiliating to be pining here in her house like this, she told herself sharply. She should get out and do something.

But she wanted to be here in case Tom came home. So she picked up a book and tried to read.

Several hours later, she heard the door rattling and she jerked awake. She had fallen asleep on the couch, and her back and neck were stiff from sleeping in an awkward position. She stumbled over to the door and looked out the window. Her heart bounded when she saw Tom at the door.

When she opened the door, he drew her into his arms. "Are you all right?" he said. "Anything happen here?"

"I'm fine. It's quiet as a church on Tuesday. What about you? How does your head feel?"

"My head feels fine." Tom's arms tightened around her, then he found her mouth in a deep kiss. Finally, he raised his head. "I've been thinking about kissing you ever since I left."

His words eased some of the pain that had tightened her chest, and she smiled at him. "Me, too."

Tom draped his arm over her shoulder and steered her into the kitchen. "I'm going to make a turkey sandwich. Do you want anything?"

"That sounds good." She hadn't realized how hungry she was. They had missed a couple of meals. "But you sit down and let me do it. Tell me what you did tonight."

"We lucked out," he said simply. "We've found someone who identified Wade and told us he rented a cabin to him. It's in the mountains in a remote location. Wade told the real estate company that he wanted to be isolated so he could do some hiking. We're going to head up there as soon as it's light. With any luck at all, we'll have him in custody before noon tomorrow."

"And then the case will be closed?"

"We have to find enough evidence to convict him. I saw Wade shoot the Steeles, but it would be nice to have some physical evidence, too." He looked up at her and said, "I'll be in Grand Springs for a while yet, Tina."

"I'm glad." It was all she could bring herself to say right now. Tom was exhausted. She could see it in his face. So she would still the questions that wanted to leap off her tongue, and try to be patient. There would be plenty of time for them to talk once Wade had been caught.

Tom stood up from the table. "Ready for bed?" he asked.

"Yes," she said in a low voice. She wanted all the time she could get with Tom. She met his gaze steadily, and desire quickened inside her when she saw the passion leap into his eyes.

Without a word he took her hand and led her up the stairs to her bedroom. They shed their clothes quickly, and Tom gathered her against him. The weariness etched into his face seemed to fall away as he bent to kiss her, and she felt herself falling into the now-familiar spiral of desire and drugging pleasure.

They tumbled onto the bed, touching and kissing as if it had been days and not mere hours since they last made love. Tina tried to pull him closer, but Tom stopped her. He pinned her hands to the bed beside her head and lifted himself to look at her.

"I can't think of anything but you, Tina. I can't concentrate on my work, because all I see is you in my head, all I feel is your skin, all I taste is your mouth."

His words gave her a fierce pleasure. She wanted to tell him she felt the same way, but couldn't find the words. So she lifted her head and kissed him instead, and he kissed her back with heat and passion, and something more. There was an urgency to his kiss, a desperation that made her respond recklessly.

In some deep part of her soul, she recognized that she wanted to bond him to her irrevocably. She didn't want Tom to forget her, or what they shared. So she curled her arms around him, holding him close. She caressed him, sliding her hands over his back, his chest, his buttocks, then drifting around to stroke the hard, hot length of him. He groaned from deep in his chest and her hand froze. But when she tried to move it, he held her against him.

"Tina," he gasped. "Tina, my love."

Her heart leaped in her chest, and the next moment he plunged into her. She curled her legs around him and held him tightly as they moved together, sensation building and finally exploding. Tom whispered her name as he poured himself into her.

They lay entwined together for a long time. Tina could feel Tom's heart, beating steadily against hers, gradually slowing down. She gloried in his weight, pressing her down into the mattress, and she traced the muscles in his back. Finally he moved to the side, tucking her close against him.

"Tina, we need to talk," he mumbled against her hair. "I need to tell you something."

She could tell he was almost asleep. "In the morning," she said, her lips brushing his chest.

But in the morning she woke to find the bed empty next to her. She sat up slowly, knowing instinctively that Tom was gone. She couldn't feel his presence in the house. There was a flash of white on the table next to her bed, and she reached for the sheet of paper.

"Got a phone call and had to leave," she read aloud. "I'll be back as soon as I can. Love, Tom."

She vaguely remembered hearing the phone ring. It had still been dark, and Tom had answered. She had fallen back to sleep with the comforting murmur of his voice surrounding her.

She got out of bed slowly and looked at the clock. She had slept too late, and it was almost time for her to get ready for work. She tried to block Tom's words from her mind. He had said they needed to talk today. She had hoped that he wanted to talk about their future, but now she wasn't so sure.

Her heart heavy, she began to get ready for work. She had always looked forward to going to the hospital, always took great pleasure in the work she did. But now all she could do was think about Tom, and wonder if they had just spent their last night together.

Chapter 15

Tom lay in the early dawn light, peering up at a cabin perched precariously on the side of a mountain. There was no sound or movement coming from the building, and no sign of Wade's truck. He wondered if Wade was even there.

He looked over at Stone Richardson, who was concealed twenty feet away from him. Bob Jones was on his other side, and both men waited for his signal to storm the cabin.

Tom had a bad feeling about this. His head still ached, a reminder of his fall onto the counter last night, but he tried to ignore it. His gut churned and he couldn't help thinking about Tina. He had hated to leave her sleeping this morning, but he had overslept and had no choice but to hurry out the door. He barely had time to scribble a note to her. As it was, Stone had teased him unmercifully on the drive to the cabin.

He couldn't help but think about the prowler she'd had outside her house. He was almost sure it was Wade, looking for him. Wade better be in this cabin, he told himself grimly. He didn't want to think what might happen if the killer slipped away from them.

His right hand tightened on his gun, and he raised his left hand in the prearranged signal to begin. The three men approached the cabin as silently as possible. Pebbles bounded down the rocks, echoing too loudly each time they bounced. He scrambled up to the door of the cabin, noting out of the corners of his eyes that Stone and Jones were right next to him.

He didn't knock on the door when he reached it. He kicked it open and swung his gun inside. "Freeze," he barked. "FBI."

There was no sound, no movement from within the cabin. He listened for several seconds, then stepped inside.

The interior was dark, and he turned on his flashlight. The small cabin was a mess. Clothes were scattered on the floor and dirty dishes sat in the sink. There was a plate of congealing eggs on the table. It looked as if the occupant had left the house in a hurry.

"He's gone." It was Bob Jones's voice, and Tom could hear the disappointment.

"Let's take another look outside. He might not have gone far."

But there was no sign of Randy Wade. Tom stood and scanned the area for a long time, looking for any signs of movement, anything that was out of place. It didn't help. Wade had slipped away from them.

"Let's take a look inside," he finally said.

Wade had indeed left in a hurry. Tom found a suitcase full of cash beneath a loose floorboard, and as he pulled it into the room, he heard Stone give a grunt of satisfaction behind him.

"We've got the bastard," Stone said, relief in his voice. He held up a gun between carefully gloved fingers. "Five will get you ten that this is the gun he used to kill the Steeles."

Tom nodded tersely. "Bag it up." He looked around the cabin. "It's going to take hours to go through everything here. Can you call your evidence technicians up here?"

Jones nodded and pulled out his radio. In a few moments he turned back to Tom. "They're on their way. It should take them about a half hour to get here."

"Good. Once they're here, we can go after Wade. He doesn't have his money, and we know what he's driving. He shouldn't be able to get far."

Tom took notes on what was in the cabin as they waited for the technicians. When they arrived, Tom stepped outside and talked to them briefly. Then he turned to Stone and Jones.

"Let's get going. I want to call Tina and make sure she's okay."

Stone frowned at him. "Why wouldn't she be?"

"I have a bad feeling about Wade," he said grimly. "I'm willing to bet a lot of money that he's the one who's been following her and prowling around her house. There was way too much coverage of my accident in the newspaper. It wouldn't have taken much detective work for Wade to find out that Tina was the nurse who took care of me."

"Let's get back to the car and call her, then," Stone said.

By the time he reached the bottom of the hill, Tom

was practically running. He reached into the car and grabbed the phone, dialing her number. She picked it up on the third ring.

"Tina?" he said. "Is everything okay?"

There was an infinitesimal pause that made him tighten his grip on the phone. "Why wouldn't it be?" she finally said.

"Wade wasn't up here in the cabin. I'm coming back to the house to check on you."

"That's not necessary," she said, and he thought he heard a thread of panic in her voice. "I'm fine and I'll be heading to work soon. I'll see you later tonight."

"Something is wrong, Tina. I can tell." Tom heard his voice rising.

"Thanks for calling," she said, and now there was no mistaking the panic. "I don't want to keep you because I know you're busy. Goodbye, Tom."

He heard the gentle click of the phone and the line went dead.

Tina set the phone carefully in its cradle and turned to the man holding the gun on her. "It was Tom," she said. "I told him everything was fine, and he's not coming back here for a while."

She prayed that it was true. *Stay away, Tom,* she whispered to herself. *Don't walk into a trap.*

Wade's face turned petulant. "I wanted him to come here. He saw me shoot the Steeles, and I have to get rid of him."

"Well, you're out of luck. He's going to be working long hours. He may not even come back here tonight."

Wade stared at her, frustration on his face. Then he

slowly smiled. "Maybe that's all right," he said. "I've got a better idea. I can kill two birds with one stone. I had to leave all my money in that cabin when I heard the police coming this morning. They thought they were so smart, sneaking up on me, but I had set some alarms for myself. I got out just in time.

"But I want my money back. Maybe your boyfriend would trade me my money for your life."

"I doubt it," she said. "The FBI doesn't negotiate with criminals."

He snorted with laughter. "When I looked through your kitchen window, I saw the way he looked at you. I'd say he'd trade plenty for you. And when he does, I'll have my chance at him. One shot and there's no more witness to the Steeles' murders."

Tina listened with horror. Wade was right. She knew Tom well enough to know that he would bargain with Wade. And if he tried to rescue her, Wade would kill him.

"Let's go, honey. You've become very valuable to me. You're my ticket out of this mess." He poked her with the gun, and she stood up. She was afraid she hadn't fooled Tom, and that he was on his way back to the house. She wanted Wade to be gone before Tom walked into a trap.

She walked out the door and got into Wade's truck without looking behind her.

Tom was out of the car before it had stopped moving. His heart pounding, he raced to the front door. It stood ajar, and terror washed over him.

"Tina?" he called, pushing the door open.

There was no answer. He listened for a moment, then stepped inside. "Tina, are you here?"

His words echoed off the floor and the ceiling. Silence.

He heard the two detectives on the steps behind him and turned around. "She's gone," he said, his voice flat.

"Maybe she just went to work," Jones said.

"Take a look in her garage. I'm betting her car is still there."

Jones turned and ran down the steps while Tom and Stone searched the house. There was no sign of Tina, but he didn't see any signs of violence, either. His fear eased a little.

"Her car is still there," Jones reported, and Tom nodded.

"Then we have to assume that Wade has her."

They scoured the town and the surrounding mountains all day and into the night, but there was no sign of Tina or Wade. It was as if they had vanished into the thin mountain air.

Urgency sharpened his fear and drove him to continue. All he could think about was Tina, alone and frightened in the mountains. The nights were becoming bitterly cold, and she didn't have a coat. He had seen her jacket hanging in the front hall closet.

At three o'clock in the morning, Stone put his hand on Tom's shoulder. "You have to take a break, Flynt," he said, but Tom could hear the sympathy in his voice. "You're not going to be any help to her if you're too exhausted to think." He jerked his head toward one of the interrogation rooms. "There's a cot in there we use when we're working late. Get a few hours of sleep."

"You and Jones haven't slept, either," he retorted.

"We're going home. We'll be back in a few hours."

Tom wanted to argue, wanted to tell Richardson he was fine, but he knew the detective was right. He needed to be alert to catch Wade. He didn't want his hands shaking from exhaustion and his mind muddled from lack of sleep. Tina's life depended on him. "All right," he said grudgingly. "I'll sleep for a few hours."

Stone slapped him on the back. "We'll be back at seven and start fresh."

Tom lay down on the cot in the dark interrogation room, but he couldn't fall asleep. He was tortured by images of Tina being held by Wade. Wade was a vicious killer, and he knew it was possible he wouldn't see her alive again.

He loved her. In the darkness of the room and in the midst of his terror, it was the one thing he saw clearly. He wanted to spend the rest of his life with Tina. He wanted to make a home with her, and a family.

He wanted to jump up from the cot and do something, right now, to find her. He couldn't bear to wait until the morning, to sleep while Tina might be suffering. But he couldn't stay awake. Against his will, he drifted off to sleep.

He woke with a jerk and sat up on the cot, wondering where he was. He stared at the institutional green of the walls and remembered, bringing his fear and desperation back in a rush.

Rolling off the cot, he pushed out of the room and into the corridor, looking around. It was very early in the morning—not yet light—and there were only a few police officers sitting at their desks. Most of them were typing up reports.

There was no sign of Richardson or Jones. Tom hurried into the detectives' room. It was deserted. He thumbed through a Rolodex on one of the desks, looking for Richardson's telephone number. He was just about to pick up the phone when the detective himself came strolling into the room.

"I figured you'd be awake already." He nodded toward the other room. "Let's get a cup of coffee. It's strong enough to take the varnish off a chair."

"Sounds good," Tom muttered.

They retreated back to the detectives' room and were talking about their strategy for the day when the telephone rang. Stone picked it up. "Richardson here."

He listened for a moment, then lunged off the desk to push a button on the telephone. Tom watched his fingers whiten as he held the receiver. Finally he said, "Here he is."

He handed Tom the phone. "Wade," he mouthed.

His heart pounding, Tom said, "This is Tom Flynt."

"Flynt, I have your girlfriend here."

Tom could hear the gloating in Wade's voice. He tried to control his rage and speak in a neutral tone of voice. "What do you want?"

"I knew you'd be reasonable." He chuckled. "Missy here told me that the FBI doesn't bargain with the likes of me, but I knew you'd be different. I saw the way you looked at her."

"What do you want, Wade?"

"I want my money back. And I want to leave this

God-forsaken town on my own, with no one follow-ing me."

"How do I know that Ms. White is still alive?" Tom wasn't sure how he managed to say the words.

"She's alive. Do you think I would kill my ace in the hole?"

"Let me talk to her." Tom's hand tightened on the receiver.

"I don't know if I can do that."

"If I don't talk to her, there's no deal."

There was a pause, then Wade said with a chuckle, "You drive a hard bargain, Flynt."

Tom could hear fumbling in the background, then Tina's voice. "Tom?"

"Tina? Are you all right? Has he hurt you?" He gripped the phone so hard that his hand hurt.

"I'm fine, Tom. He hasn't touched me."

"Are you warm enough?"

"We're in a cabin..."

Tina's voice stopped abruptly. Then Wade came back on the line. "That's all you're going to get, Flynt. Now do I get my money back, or does Ms. White go home in a box?"

"You'll get your money," Tom said grimly. "Where and when do you want to make the exchange?"

"Nine o'clock this evening. I don't want to leave during the day. It makes it so much easier for your friends in the police department to follow me. So we'll make sure it's dark before we do our business."

"All right." Tom ground his teeth at the thought of Tina being in danger for another twelve hours. "Where?"

"I think we'll meet at the place where you had

your accident. I have a fondness for that spot." He chuckled again. "Do you think you can remember where that was?"

"I'll be there, Wade. And you'd better be, too. If you touch one hair of Ms. White's head, you're going to die."

"You're letting your emotions get in the way of business, Flynt. And that's all this is. Business. I need that money, and you apparently need Ms. White. I'll see you tonight at nine."

The line went dead, and Tom turned to Stone. "Could you trace the call?"

Stone shook his head. "He was using a cell phone. We can narrow it down, but that's about all."

"I saw you press a button. Did you record him?"

Stone nodded. "Let's listen to it again. Maybe we'll get a clue."

But the only clue they had was that Tina had said she was in a cabin. "There are hundreds of cabins in the mountains," Stone said, slumping into a chair. "That doesn't narrow it down at all."

He lifted his head and looked over at Tom. "I have another idea. It may sound nuts to you, but hear me out."

He leaned forward and began to speak. Tom narrowed his eyes, but he didn't interrupt. Finally, when Stone stopped speaking, Tom shrugged. "You're right, it sounds nuts, but I'm willing to try anything."

Stone picked up the phone and made a call, and a half hour later, an attractive young blond woman walked into the room. Stone jumped up and reached for her, pulling her to him for a quick kiss. Then, with his arm around her shoulders, he said, "This is my wife, Jessica. Jessica, this is Tom Flynt. He's the FBI agent I told you about.''

Jessica Richardson held out her hand and gave him a warm smile. ''I'm so glad you regained your memory, Mr. Flynt. And I'm very sorry about what's happened to Tina. I hope I can help you find her.''

''I hope so, too.''

Jessica smiled at him. ''You look skeptical.''

He shrugged. ''It sounds pretty odd.''

''I agree. But you never know.''

''Jessica had visions, for lack of a better word, of a murder we had here in Grand Springs a few years ago. She was instrumental in helping us solve the case.''

Jessica blushed. ''Stone did the work. I was glad to be able to help.''

Tom leaned forward. ''Your husband suggested that you might be able to listen to the tape we made of Wade and Tina and get an idea where they might be. Do you think that's possible?''

''I don't know, Mr. Flynt,'' she said frankly. ''I haven't really had any 'visions' since that time. But I'm certainly willing to try.''

Tom sat back in his chair and watched her. ''Whenever you're ready, Mrs. Richardson.''

''Go ahead.''

Tom played the tape, and watched Jessica Richardson as she concentrated. Her eyes took on a faraway look, and she appeared to look inside herself. When the tape was finished, she sat without moving for what seemed like a long time. Tom wanted to ask her if she had seen anything, but he forced himself to keep quiet.

Finally she turned to him, a look of distress on her

face. "I could see a cabin, but I know that doesn't help much. It looks as if it's tucked under a huge rock. It's so well-hidden that it's barely visible." She turned her palms up. "I can't see anything else. But I don't think it's near the city. It felt very isolated."

Tom swallowed his fear and his frustration and nodded. "Thanks, Mrs. Richardson. We really appreciate the effort."

"Please, call me Jessica." He could see the distress in her eyes. "Will you let me listen to the tape again, by myself? I might be able to come up with more."

"Go right ahead." Tom stood up and waited for Stone to say goodbye to his wife, then the two of them left the room. As they shut the door, Tom could hear Wade's voice on the tape recorder.

Just then Bob Jones came hurrying down the corridor. "I got in touch with both the cell phone companies in town. One of them was able to verify that the call came from their phone. And they could tell us which tower it was relayed from. It doesn't tell us where she is, but it narrows it down."

Tom wanted to grab the older detective and kiss him. "Good work, Jones. Where is this tower?"

Jones pointed to the map that hung on the wall behind them. It included Grand Springs and a wide section of the mountains surrounding it. "Right about here. They said they have towers every three or four miles in that area. So this is the area where we should be looking."

Jones drew a line around what looked like a dauntingly large area. And Tom knew that it was mountainous. "How many people can we get to search the area?" he asked.

"We'll put every available officer on it," Jones said promptly. "I'll start making the calls."

"Take my cell phone," Stone said. "If Jessica comes up with anything, she'll call you."

"Thanks," Tom said quietly.

"Listen to me," Stone said, laying his hand on Tom's arm. "If you find anything, don't be a hot dog. Call for backup, and wait for help. Don't be a hero."

"Don't worry. I won't let anything happen to Tina."

Stone shook his head. "That's not what I meant, and you know it. Listen to me. I'll get another phone from the department and make sure you have the number. Call if you see or hear anything."

"I know the drill, Richardson."

"Then see that you follow it."

Tom didn't bother to answer. He raced for his car, making sure he had Stone's cell phone and a jug of water. He didn't wait to find out where everyone else was going to search. He'd cover the whole area, on foot, by himself, if necessary. He would find Tina if it were the last thing he ever did.

Seven hours later, at three o'clock in the afternoon, he was in the mountains outside Grand Springs, about an hour away. The air was cold, but the sun beat down mercilessly on Tom's face. His head throbbed and his eyes ached. He hadn't seen one cabin that looked like the one Jessica Richardson described. He had seen a number of shacks that looked abandoned, and he'd looked in every one of them. But time was running short and he had a huge area left to cover.

As he was walking along, he stepped into a depression in the earth and stumbled. As he reached for a tree to steady himself, he realized that he had come across an old, abandoned road. The depression he'd stumbled into was a tire rut.

His gaze sharpened as he looked at the road. It was overgrown with weeds, and small saplings sprouted between the ruts. But someone had driven over this road very recently. Some of the saplings were snapped off and there was fresh dirt exposed in the tire tracks.

He tried to beat down the excitement as he followed the road higher up the mountain. It could mean nothing, he told himself. But the road could lead to Wade's hideout.

He flipped open his phone and called Stone. He explained what he'd found and told him where he was. "I'm following the road. I'll let you know if it looks promising."

"I'm going to head in that direction," Stone replied. "I'll be there as soon as I can."

Tom slipped the phone back into his pocket and turned it off. He didn't want it ringing and alerting Wade that he was in the area. He hiked higher and higher, following the tracks, and his excitement grew. Tina could be just ahead.

Finally the road turned a corner into an open meadow. He immediately stepped back into the trees and scanned the meadow in front of him.

He almost missed the cabin. It was tiny and practically falling apart, its weathered brown boards blending almost perfectly into the trees. A cliff bordered one side of the meadow, and Tom's heart sped up when he saw that the cabin was tucked into a massive rock overhang. This looked very much like the place Jessica Richardson had described.

Tom stood for a while, deciding on the best approach. He finally slipped through the trees to the cliff behind the cabin. Moving slowly, he was able to edge close enough to the cabin that he could hear a voice coming from inside.

His heart pounding, he listened for a while. It was Wade! He had found them!

Chapter 16

His heart thundered painfully in his chest, and Tom had to force himself to remain motionless. If Wade was talking to someone, it must mean Tina was in this cabin. And more importantly, she was still alive. He ached to run inside and pull her into his arms.

He loved her. It was painfully clear to him. And he couldn't bear the thought that she was in danger.

But he took a deep breath and waited until his heart slowed down. If he rushed into the cabin now, it would be a disaster. He had to utilize his training, and think logically and calmly in order to help Tina. He had to put aside the personal, shut down all his emotions.

He closed his eyes until he had erased the picture of Tina from his mind. Then he looked around. The first thing he had to do was warn Stone. He was on his way to the cabin. It would be a disaster if he came bursting into the meadow and warned Wade that he'd been found.

Tom backed away from the cabin, moving slowly even though all his instincts screamed at him to hurry. It had been thirty-six hours since Wade kidnapped Tina—the longest thirty-six hours of his life. When he was finally back in the shelter of the trees, he retreated until he was sure Wade wouldn't be able to hear him speaking. Then he turned on his phone and told Stone what he had found.

"Wait until some backup gets there," Stone urged. "Don't do anything stupid."

"I won't. I'm not going to risk Tina's life. But I don't want you to come charging into the meadow. Our only advantage right now is that Wade doesn't know we've found him."

"We'll be careful. Keep in touch if you can."

"Will do." Tom turned off the phone again and slipped it back into his pocket. He wouldn't be using it again until he had Wade in custody.

Moving carefully, he maneuvered himself back into position near the cabin. Shadows were lengthening in the meadow—the cliff was blocking the rays of the sun, and it wouldn't be long before the entire meadow was plunged into darkness. Night came suddenly and swiftly in the mountains. Once it was dark, he had to move quickly before Wade left for their meeting.

As the shadows crept over the cabin, he edged toward a window. Wade's voice drifted through the broken glass, sounding frighteningly normal. Occasionally it was muffled, as if Wade had bent down. The next time it happened, Tom risked a quick look inside.

Tina lay on a narrow cot, her hands and feet bound

and her mouth covered with a piece of silver tape. Rage swept over him as he looked at her, helpless. He dropped down below the window again and silently promised her that Wade would be punished for what he had done to her.

As darkness crept over the meadow, Tom saw a light flare on inside the cabin. He frowned with surprise. There were no electric lines leading to this isolated meadow.

Then he heard the growl of a generator, coming from behind the building. He smiled with grim satisfaction. "I have you now, Wade," he whispered to himself.

It took longer than he expected to move to the rear of the cabin. Light was disappearing quickly, and he didn't want to alert Wade by stepping on a rock or a stick. Any noise in the isolated meadow would reverberate far too loudly in the silence. By the time he reached the generator, night had fallen in the meadow.

It only took moments to disable the generator. It clanked a couple of times, then ground to a halt. The lights in the cabin went out, plunging everything in the area into darkness.

Tom was betting that it wouldn't take long for Wade to come out of the cabin to check on the generator. It would be far safer for Tina if he arrested Wade out in the open, rather than in the confines of the cabin. So Tom retreated into the shadows and waited.

Within a few minutes, he heard the door of the cabin open. He tensed, but Wade didn't appear. Had he gone around the other way?

Then a bobbing light appeared, and Tom realized that Wade had a flashlight. Tom shrank away from the thin beam of light and waited until Wade was bending over the generator.

He had his gun in his hand before he stood up and ran over to his target. "Freeze, Wade. FBI."

Wade spun around, a look of disbelief on his face. Suddenly, he raised the flashlight and swung it toward Tom's head. When Tom put up his arm to block the blow, the heavy light hit his arm, sending pain shooting up to his shoulder.

Before Tom could recover, Wade reached under his arm and pulled out a gun. Tom leaped toward him, grabbing his arm and keeping the gun pointed away from them.

"You're going to die, Flynt," Wade panted. "And then your girlfriend will die, too. But not until I've had some fun with her. She's a looker, isn't she?"

Rage gave Tom strength he didn't know he had. He kept Wade's gun pointed away from him while he brought his own gun up and pointed it at Wade's chest. "Wade, drop the gun now, or I'll have to shoot you."

After a tense few moments, Wade dropped his own gun and Tom kicked it away from them. Tom slowly let him go and held the weapon steady on Wade. "All right, down on the ground and put your hands on top of your head."

Instead of obeying, Wade lunged for Tom, grabbing for his gun at the same time. Tom read the desperation in the other man's jerky movements and knew that Wade had nothing left to lose. He had already killed four people. He wouldn't hesitate to kill him and Tina.

Wade's hand wrapped around Tom's gun as they struggled in grim silence. Wade was unbelievably strong. Tom felt him pushing the gun away from him, trying to aim it toward Tom. He swept out his leg, trying to trip Wade and knock him off balance. Wade stumbled and the gun went off.

The single shot echoed in the darkness, and Tom felt Wade fall backwards. He crumbled to the ground, and Tom grabbed his flashlight and shone it down on him.

Blood oozed from a wound in his chest, and Wade lay very still. Tom put his fingers on Wade's neck. There was no pulse. Wade was dead.

Tom slowly straightened, looking down at Wade's body. He felt a brief flicker of grief at the waste of a life, but he knew he'd had no choice. If he hadn't shot Wade, he would have been killed himself. Along with Tina.

Holstering his gun, he turned and ran into the cabin, calling Tina's name. Tina had managed to sit up on the bed, and she was watching the door, fear in her eyes. When she heard him, she slumped back against the wall.

Tom eased the tape away from her mouth. "Are you all right?" he asked, as he fumbled with the string that bound her hands.

"I'm fine. Just a little sore." She rubbed at her wrists, and he could see angry red lines circling them.

"You're safe now. Wade's dead."

Her eyes filled with tears. "I heard the gunshot. I knew you were out there because I recognized your voice, and I was so afraid that he'd shot you."

Tom tossed aside the rope that had been binding her legs and pulled her into his arms. "You're not going to get rid of me that easily."

She clung to him, holding him tightly. He could

feel her shaking, and he sat down on the cot and pulled her into his lap. "It's over, sweetheart. And I'm so sorry that you had to suffer like this."

"It's not your fault," she said into his shoulder. "Wade is the one to blame."

"I should have made sure you had police protection," he said, his voice grim. "And believe me, I won't forgive myself for a long time."

At that she lifted her head. "Don't be stupid, Tom. It wasn't your fault that Wade kidnapped me."

She was looking steadily at him, and even in the darkness he could see the conviction in her eyes. "You're way too generous," he muttered, and then he found her mouth with his. He had to kiss her, taste her, assure himself that she was alive and unharmed.

She melted into his kiss, straining to move closer to him. But before he could lose control, he eased himself away from her. "Are you sure you're all right?"

She nodded. "I'm fine now."

"What happened? How did he get to you?"

"He cut out a pane of glass in one of the panels by the front door, then reached inside and let himself in. I was upstairs and I never heard him. I walked down into the kitchen and there he was. He had a gun."

"I knew something was wrong when I called. I could hear it in your voice."

"I was trying so hard to sound normal. He wanted you to come back to the house, and I didn't want you to walk into a trap."

"Better that than the thirty-six hours you've endured," he said grimly. He couldn't stop himself from touching her face again, just to assure himself that she was all right.

He saw her wistful smile in the darkness. "It sounds like we were both trying to protect each other."

"It's my job to protect you." Emotion made his voice gruff. "Believe me, this won't happen again."

Tina eased away from him and stood up. "Shouldn't you call the Grand Springs police and tell them what happened?"

Tom frowned at her, wondering at her sudden coolness. But she was right. Stone Richardson was waiting to hear from him. "I guess I should."

Tina watched as Tom took his cell phone out of his pocket and dialed. After a moment, he began speaking in a low voice. She looked around the cabin, now nothing more than dark shadowy shapes, and shuddered. It would be a long time before she forgot what had happened here.

But Tom had rescued her. She knew full well that Randy Wade hadn't intended to let her go, or Tom, either. He'd bragged to her about what he planned for the exchange. He'd intended to ambush Tom, killing the only witness to his murder of the Steeles. He hadn't told her so, but she knew he would then kill her, too. Wade was a desperate man and couldn't afford to leave any witnesses.

Tom snapped the phone closed and turned back to her. "Stone and Bob Jones will be here in a few minutes. They're on the old road I found, just around the curve."

"What will happen now?" she asked.

Tom shrugged. "There will be lots of questions to answer and lots of paperwork to do. It'll take a while to wrap up this case, since there were several crimes involved. We'll have to check the gun we found in Wade's last cabin and make sure it was the one that he used to kill the Steeles and the two men he killed in the bank robbery. And I'll have to explain why I shot him.''

''But if you hadn't, he would have killed both of us!''

Tom reached out and swept her into his arms again. ''I know, sweetheart. It's just a formality. But the Bureau requires it every time an agent uses deadly force.''

She soaked up the comfort from Tom's embrace, unwilling to let him go. She was going to have to do that soon enough.

After a moment, Tom stepped away from her. ''I hear Richardson and Jones. Do you want me to have an officer take you home? I might be here for a while.''

His words made an arrow of pain quiver in her heart. ''Whatever is easiest for you.''

He looked outside. ''You probably want to go home. Let me have someone take you there. I'll be back as soon as I can.''

''Take your time,'' she said, feeling hot tears pool in her eyes. ''I understand.''

He kissed her once more, then led her out the door into the now completely dark meadow. There were two shadowy figures, holding flashlights, walking toward them.

''You okay, Ms. White?''

Tina recognized Bob Jones's voice. ''I'm fine,'' she said.

"Is there a uniformed officer on the road?" Tom asked. "I'd like someone to take Tina home."

"I'll get someone up here right away." Stone spoke into his radio, and all Tina could hear was a crackle of static. "It'll be just a moment," he said to her. "I know you've had a rough time, but we'll need to ask you some questions. Can we come by in the morning?"

"Of course," she replied. She turned to look for Tom, but he was standing with Bob Jones next to the cabin, deep in conversation. This was his job, she reminded herself. He didn't have time to hold her hand.

She understood that, but the distance between them was still painful. His case was over, and Tom would be leaving Grand Springs. Oh, he would be around for a few more days, tying up loose ends and making sure everything was taken care of. But his job here was finished, and he would be returning to his home.

And she didn't even know where that was, she thought with a pang. His family lived in Chicago, but she didn't know where he was based. It was just one of the many things she didn't know about him.

Her legs felt leaden as she walked toward the road. Tom was right. She needed a hot bath and about twenty-four hours of sleep. She stumbled once and caught herself just before she fell.

"Tina, wait," she heard Tom call behind her, "someone will walk you down to the car."

"I'm fine," she called back over her shoulder, forcing herself to smile. "You're all busy, and the car will be here in a moment."

She felt Tom watching her but didn't turn around.

He had work to do. And she needed to get used to the fact that he wasn't going to be around.

It was late the next morning when she heard a key turn in the front door lock. She'd been sitting in the kitchen, drinking coffee and staring out the window, and she stood up and walked into the living room.

"Hi, Tina," Tom said quietly. He came over and wrapped his arms around her, giving her a kiss. "I'm sorry I didn't call last night. How are you feeling?"

"Pretty good," she said, drinking in the sight of him. His hair was disheveled and there were lines of exhaustion on his face. But his eyes were clear, and there wasn't a hint of pain in them. "How about you?"

"I'm fine." He kissed her again. "I don't suppose there's any food in there?"

"There is still some turkey left. How about a sandwich?"

"Sounds wonderful."

She poured him a cup of coffee, and then made him a sandwich. It was a good excuse to not look at him. She was afraid he would see the sorrow in her eyes, and she didn't want anything to mar their last days together.

"What's wrong, Tina?" he asked softly.

Startled, she spun around to face him. "What do you mean?"

"You look sad. And you looked that way last night, too." He got up from his chair and came over to stand next to her, taking her hand. "It was the violence, wasn't it?"

"What do you mean?" She was genuinely confused.

"Wade kidnapped you at gunpoint, he tied you up and threatened to kill you. It must have brought back awful memories of your life with your father."

"Oh, Tom." She melted inside and gave him an impulsive hug. "Thank you for worrying about me. But I didn't think about my father at all. I was scared, but no more than anyone else would have been."

She tried to ease herself away from his embrace, but he tightened his arms around her. "What is it, then? Are you upset that I couldn't come home with you last night?"

"Of course not! That's your job. I knew you had to stay."

"Then what is it?" He touched her mouth with his finger when she would have spoken. "And don't tell me nothing is wrong. I know you better than that. I thought we promised to be honest with one another."

She didn't want to tell him why she was sad, but he was right. They *had* promised to be honest with each other. She could give him that, at least.

"Your case is finished," she said in a low voice. "You don't belong in Grand Springs. I know you're going to be leaving. I'm not looking forward to that."

She lifted her head and met his gaze, seeing astonishment in his brown eyes. "You thought I was going to just walk away from Grand Springs and you?"

She shrugged. "You can't stay here. As far as I know, there isn't an FBI office in Grand Springs."

His eyes softened as he watched her. "I keep forgetting that this is all new to you," he murmured. Then he grinned, and she saw a devilish sparkle in his eyes. "You're right, I am leaving town. I've been undercover on this case for several months. I have some time off, and I want to see my family and let them know I'm all right.''

He bent and kissed her thoroughly, and she felt passion stirring in him. In spite of herself, she felt an answering leap inside of her. Then he lifted his head.

''I don't want to visit my family by myself, Tina. Will you come with me? I want to introduce you to my parents—as my bride.''

''What?'' She wasn't sure she had heard him correctly.

''I love you, Tina. Will you marry me?''

She felt the tears prickle in her eyes. ''Of course, I'll marry you,'' she whispered. ''I love you, too, Tom.''

Then she couldn't say anything more. He covered her mouth with his and she melted against him. When he lifted his head, he was breathing deeply and his eyes glittered with need. Without a word, he swept her into his arms and carried her upstairs to her bed.

They fell together on the bed, trying to pull off their clothes without letting go of each other. He kissed her with a hunger that she recognized, because it consumed her, too. Their hands flew over each other, touching, caressing, holding. She couldn't get enough of him. And when he plunged into her, she rose to meet him, wrapping her arms and legs around him and whispering his name.

They lay tangled together on the bed for a long time. When he wanted to roll to the side, she held him tightly against her, relishing the weight of his body on hers. Finally, when her heart rate had slowed to normal and her body was limp and sated, she turned her head and kissed him once more.

He rolled to the side and gathered her close. Pressing his mouth to her temple, he murmured, "I want to get married right away."

"Me, too," she said without opening her eyes.

He eased away from her, then she felt him watching her.

"Are you sure?" he asked, raising himself on one elbow. "I don't want to rush you into anything."

"You don't?" She trailed a finger down his ribs, then grinned up at him. "That wasn't the impression I had a few minutes ago."

"A few minutes ago, I would have died if we hadn't made love," he said, grinning back. "That was an emergency situation."

"I see." She stretched and smiled at him, happier than she'd ever been in her life. "I can see that the concept of emergencies is going to take on a whole new meaning in my life."

"You'd better believe it." He pounced on her again, kissing her until she felt desire stirring again. Then he sat up, pulling her with him.

"I'm serious, Tina. I want to marry you as soon as possible. But you may want to have a fancy wedding with all of the trimmings."

"That's not important to me," she said. "I don't care about putting on a big show. I just want us to be together."

He kissed her again. "That's all that matters to me. I'm based in the Bureau's St. Louis office right now. Do you want me to apply for a transfer to the Denver office? It will be a long commute between Denver and Grand Springs, but I'm willing to do it."

Her heart melted all over again. "That's not necessary, Tom. I'm sure there are hospitals in St. Louis that need nurses. I'll find a job there."

"I know how attached you are to this house, and how much it means to you. You've lived in Grand Springs all your life. It doesn't seem fair to ask you to give this up."

"We'll keep the house and visit Grand Springs regularly. But my life is with you, not in this house. You are what makes me happy. I'll miss my friends in Grand Springs, but it's not as if I'll never see them again."

Tom took her hands and bent forward to kiss her. "Then let's get married right away. We've already started a tradition of spending the holidays together. Let's continue it as husband and wife." His eyes gleamed at her. "And think about the traditions we could start under the Christmas tree."

"I can hardly wait."

"Then let's start right now." Tom wrapped her in his arms, and Tina saw the future unfolding in front of her, bright and full of happiness.

* * * * *

Watch for the next installment of
36 HOURS—
*when romance ignites between
three couples
who meet during
a tumultuous holiday party in*

36 HOURS: THE CHRISTMAS
THAT CHANGED EVERYTHING

With stories by

Mary Lynn Baxter
Marilyn Pappano
Christine Flynn

Coming to you only
from Silhouette Books
in November 2000

And now for a sneak preview of
36 HOURS: THE CHRISTMAS
THAT CHANGED EVERYTHING
please turn the page.

Chapter 1

The party was a drag.

But then what had he expected? Shane McCoy peered at his pointed-toed boots in order to hide his annoyance. He hadn't planned to attend this community-wide event; social functions of this nature weren't to his liking. But for some reason, he'd let his neighboring rancher cajole him into showing up.

Maybe he'd felt the need to reacquaint himself with Grand Springs and the people in it. He'd been back to his hometown in Colorado over a year now and for the most part, he'd kept to himself.

Or maybe his friend had been able to twist his arm because it was the Christmas season, a time not to be antisocial. More than that, it was a time not to be alone. And he was a loner, which didn't bother him in the least. Shane had learned long ago not to let people's opinions affect him, holding on to the old adage that what anyone else said about him wasn't *his* business.

Shane swallowed a sigh before turning his attention to what was going on around him. People were milling about with drinks in hand, talking and laughing.

He had to admit that as far as parties went, this one sponsored by the Grand Springs Chamber of Commerce held in Randolph's Restaurant, a popular eating place, was well done. A huge tree dominated one corner of the banquet hall that was located in the rear. The fir was decorated with what looked to be a million sparkling ornaments and ablaze with the same number of white lights. In addition, bright red poinsettias were arranged in clusters about the room.

A festive environment. A festive time. So again, why did he feel so disjointed, so out of place? Shane shifted from one foot to the other, wishing he were back at his ranch.

Swallowing another sigh, Shane focused his attention on a couple on the dance floor whom he'd met once in his banker's office—Steve Wilson, a local doctor, and his wife, Rebecca.

He also recognized another couple whom he'd been introduced to not long ago. Lucas Harding, vice president of a major corporation, and his secretary, Sarah Lewis, were together at the goodie table, heaping their plates full.

Close by was Jake Williams, his rancher friend, who was holding court in the midst of several other men. Shane could hear their laughter from where he stood.

Deciding he'd remained antisocial long enough, Shane pushed away from the wall and was about to make his way over to Jake when he pulled up short, both mentally and physically.

He blinked, then blinked again. Nah, it wasn't her. Even so, he couldn't look away. That was when he realized he hadn't made a mistake. It was her—Julie Harrison, a longtime friend.

The bottom dropped out of his stomach when he noticed something else: she was pregnant.

It had been several years since their paths had crossed. He recalled that it was after Julie had married and he had run into her at a restaurant.

During the brief encounter, Julie had been her warm, cordial self, but the shadows in those exquisite dark-blue eyes hadn't escaped him.

But then, nothing about Julie had ever escaped him. He'd been in love with her all his life, or so it seemed. However, that was a secret he'd never shared with anyone, certainly not her.

They had grown up together as neighbors in Grand Springs. And because he was only two years older than she was, they had run in the same crowd at school and moved in the same social circles outside of school as well.

He'd had every intention of turning their friendship into something more, but then she had started going out with his best friend. Much to Shane's chagrin, that relationship had endured until Julie left for college where she met her husband.

Thinking of her husband forced Shane's thoughts back to the present, back to Julie, who was talking to a woman who appeared to be a close friend.

Shane's eyes greedily soaked up how lovely Julie looked, lovelier than ever now that she was pregnant. If only things had turned out differently, that would be his child growing inside her. If only he'd said something to her that night he'd kissed her....

"Damn," he muttered, refusing to dwell on the past and what might have been. Anyhow, it was too late for them. He had a full life, despite the loneliness that dogged him at times.

And it wasn't as though he was alone in the world. He wasn't. He had his mother and sister who lived in Denver. When the loneliness became unbearable, he either went to see them or invited them for a visit, especially his sister, whose husband and twin boys loved to come to the ranch. It was just the season making him feel out of sorts.

As for Julie—well, she was probably in the best of holiday spirits. After all, she had a baby on the way to love and care for. And a husband lurking in the wings, Shane reminded himself harshly.

Still he found himself unable to take his eyes off her.

INTIMATE MOMENTS ® *Silhouette* ®

presents the gripping miniseries

*WHERE TIME IS
OF THE ESSENCE
IN THE SEARCH
FOR TRUE LOVE....*

CINDERELLA FOR A NIGHT—on sale Sept. 2000
by **Susan Mallery** (IM #1029)

A THANKSGIVING TO REMEMBER—on sale Oct. 2000
by **Margaret Watson** (IM #1035)

A VERY...PREGNANT NEW YEAR'S—on sale Dec. 2000
by **Doreen Roberts** (IM #1047)

MY SECRET VALENTINE—on sale Jan. 2001
by **Marilyn Pappano** (IM #1053)

Don't miss an original
Silhouette Christmas anthology
**36 HOURS: THE CHRISTMAS
THAT CHANGED EVERYTHING**
with stories by
Mary Lynn Baxter, Marilyn Pappano, Christine Flynn
On sale November 2000

Available at yor favorite retail outlet.

Silhouette ®
Where love comes alive ™

You're not going to believe this offer!

In October and November 2000, buy any two Harlequin or Silhouette books and save $10.00 off future purchases, or buy any three and save $20.00 off future purchases!

Just fill out this form and attach 2 proofs of purchase (cash register receipts) from October and November 2000 books and Harlequin will send you a coupon booklet worth a total savings of $10.00 off future purchases of Harlequin and Silhouette books in 2001. Send us 3 proofs of purchase and we will send you a coupon booklet worth a total savings of $20.00 off future purchases.

Saving money has never been this easy.

I accept your offer! Please send me a coupon booklet:

Name: _____

Address: _____ City: _____

State/Prov.: _____ Zip/Postal Code: _____

Optional Survey!

INTIMATE MOMENTS ®

™ *Silhouette* ®

COMING NEXT MONTH